# Finn and the Wild Goose

Sammy Horner

23 22 21 20 7 6 5 4 3 2 1

First published 2020 by Sarah Grace Publishing,
an imprint of Malcolm Down Publishing Ltd.
www.malcolmdown.co.uk



British Library Cataloguing in Publication Data
A catalogue record for this book is available from the British Library.

ISBN 978-1-912863-60-0

Cover illustration by Mary Fleeson
Inside illustrations by Sanoji Rathnasekara
Additional design by Mark Fleeson
Art direction by Sarah Grace
Author photo by Kylie Horner

Printed in the UK

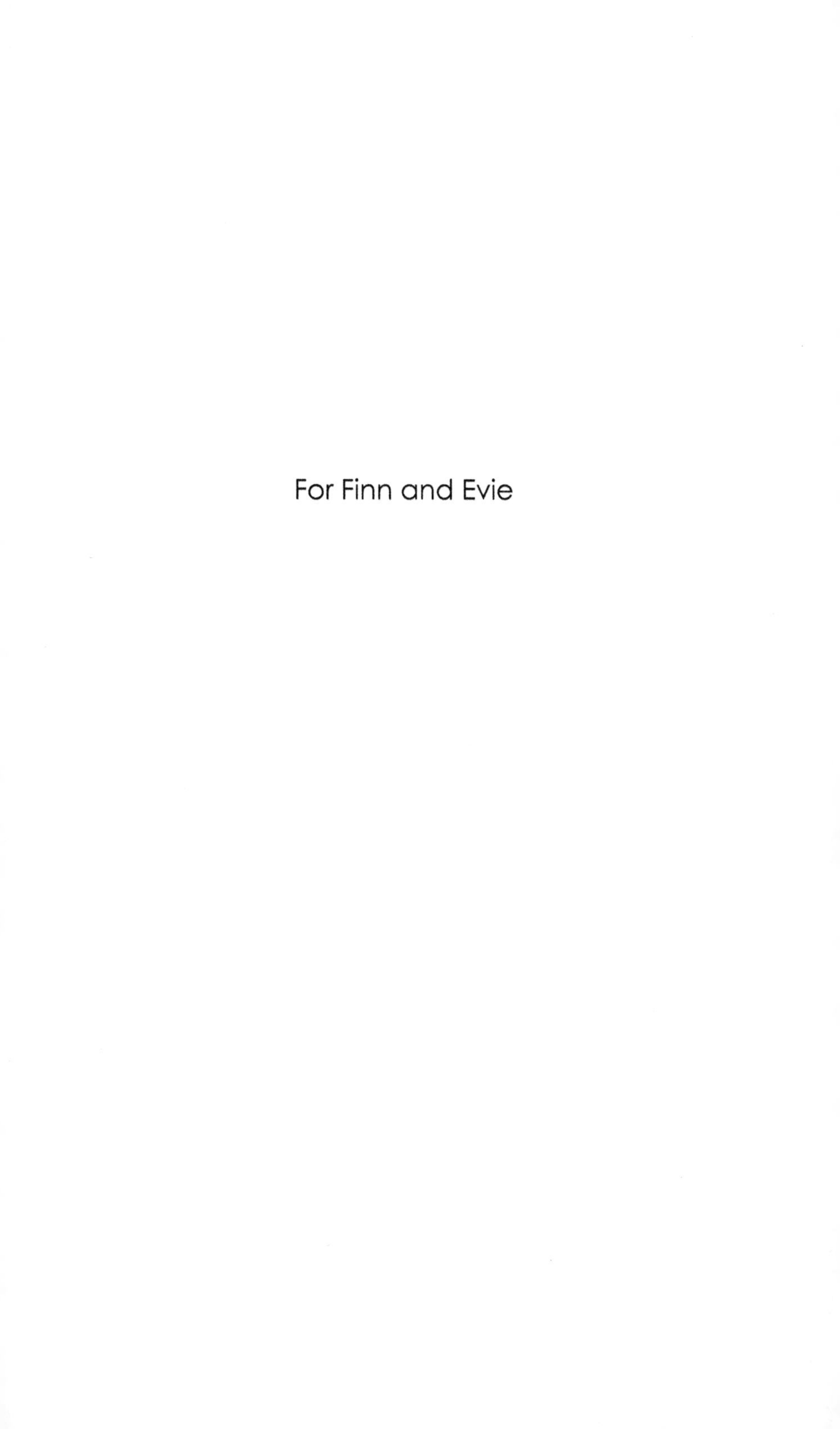

For Finn and Evie

## What others are saying about *Finn and the Wild Goose . . .*

*Finn and the Wild Goose* is a lyrical and beautifully woven story of Irish folklore, family, love and acceptance. Magical, and a highly recommended read for all ages.

Cat Hogan, *Irish Times* bestseller list author of *They All Fall Down* and *There Was A Crooked Man*

An enchanting wander through Irish mythology.

Bob Hartman, acclaimed children's performance storyteller and author of bestselling *Lion Storyteller Bible*, among many others.

Rich in the lore of Ireland, *Finn and the Wild Goose* is a grand quest for children and adults alike. Samuel Horner, storyteller extraordinaire, crafts this novel with the flavour of the Irish fairytale of Fionn MacCumhail in a modern setting. When sister Evie is kidnapped, seven-year-old Finn Cannon must undertake a quest to rescue her.

This journey has greater depth than a mere fairytale. It touches on profound truths sought by the heart of mankind. As one of the main characters, Granda, puts it: "There is another story that instructs us in the way of true peace. . . It is the one that I choose freely and the one that I will pass on to my children and my children's children!" Five stars.

Suzy Parish, Author of *Flowers From Afghanistan*

In my many years of musically collaborating with Sammy Horner, I've known him to be a wry, thoughtful lyricist. His music has a smile in it, although he's capable of bringing sorrow and reckoning across as well. Having read *Finn and The Wild Goose*, I don't know why I was so taken aback with the pure poetry of his prose, but my jaw dropped, and the sense of listening to a great storyteller overwhelmed me. Sam has a heart of gold, spun by the Spirit in some Celtic tale. His words are generous and loving, wise and wonderful, and this story is uniquely his.

Phil Madeira, Nashville Musician and Author of *God On The Rocks*

This is a beautifully written quest that will dig deep into your soul and make your imagination dance – a wonderfully rich story for children and adults.

Sammy Horner has been telling stories for years – whether in song or sat in the corner of a cosy bar. There's always laughter, honesty, questions, mystery, a sense of the ridiculous and something much deeper going on beneath the surface. This book has got all of that - and more. Drawing on his celtic roots, Sammy brings to life a myriad of colourful characters for a quest, and whilst it's most definitely away with fairies, it is also much closer to home than we think.

Sean Stillman, Author of *God's Biker: Motorcycle & Misfits*

## Chapter One

# 'Diddly-Dum'

Big grey clouds splashed across the sky as the ferry skimmed through the Irish Sea, leaving Scotland behind. A lady's strong Scottish accent blared through the ship's speaker system letting drivers and passengers know that it was time to get back in their vehicles. Her voice came out all tinny and muffled, like a robot on a bad TV show.

Finn loved the ferry. He got to drink hot chocolate and lounge in the big seats, watching through the little windows as the boat tipped the ever-moving horizon. Mum wasn't much fun on ferries. She always went quiet and looked a bit green, but Finn and his dad thought it was funny to watch the other passengers trying to walk in a straight line. When a big wave hit, they would go toppling into each other like skittles.

With land in sight, the family joined the queue of other people filing down the narrow metal staircase into the belly of the boat, where their car was waiting for them.

Finn clicked his seatbelt into place. Ah, that satisfying *clunk*! It was the sound of adventures beginning. Dad fumbled with the buckle on two-year-old Evie's car seat, making her giggle and wriggle so that her freckled face flushed pink and her curly red hair went all 'volcano head'. Mum turned round from the front seat to grin at them. She looked a more normal colour now. "All aboard Big Red," she said, as Dad pushed the car into gear. Everybody was tired but excited. Evie was doubly excited, because Evie was always excited. As the engine settled into her familiar purr, Mum inserted a USB stick – in the shape of a little laughing leprechaun – into the car music system. She had made a playlist of her favourite Irish songs just for the trip. She called it her 'Diddly-Dum' music.

"It's important that we get in the mood," she said, as the car was filled with the sound of furious fiddling.

This kind of music always made Mum a little nutty and sure enough, within seconds, her wild blonde hair was lashing around like spaghetti in a hurricane. Dad rolled his eyes, but in no time, he was singing along, his knees jumping to the rhythm of the reels and jigs. Evie joined in with the singing too. She couldn't really speak properly yet, but she sang, head back, red curls wildly dancing about her head, eyes closed, and arms outstretched. It was something that sounded like, "*OHHH BAA DAA BO!*" at full volume, over and over again.

Finn watched his mum's mop of hair flick and flop as her head rocked wildly from side to side. The music seemed to fill every space in the car, but then it suddenly changed from blattering bodhráns[1],

1. Bodhrán, pronounced 'Bow-raun' – An Irish drum.

wind-powered whistles and fiery fiddles to a soft gentle moan. It seemed to be coming from Mum, who wasn't shaking her hair anymore. Finn felt strangely uneasy. Why had Mum stopped jigging about so suddenly, and what had happened to the music? The moan then morphed into a cry, then a wail that made Finn shiver as though he had a chill.

"Mum! What's wrong? Mum! Why are you . . ." Finn's question was cut short as his mum turned her head to face him. As she twisted around, Finn saw eyes staring at him through thick white hair. Not the eyes of his mother, but dark, black eyes that stared right through him. The woman's mouth was framed in scarlet red lips, from which came a low, mournful wail.

Finn's eyes bugged out like he was some kind of frog-boy. The woman's mouth, (this was no longer Finn's mother), kept opening wider and wider until a terrible scream came from deep within her. Suddenly she reached out with long thin fingers to grab Finn. Frozen in fear, a scream suspended in his throat and then . . . *BANG!*

Finn shook his head and rubbed his eyes. What had happened?

Once again, Mum and Evie were singing to 'Diddly-Dum' music. He stared at his mother. Yes, it was definitely Mum. No sign of that other strange woman. Finn took a deep breath and laughed to himself. A dream? Yes, he must have fallen asleep and not even realised. He'd been woken by the loud bang of the ferry doors swinging open. Now the car was bouncing over the big metal ramps that led them out of the open jaws onto Ireland's solid ground.

## Chapter Two

# Soda Bread and Plum Trees

Every time Finn came to Ireland, he could see why it was called the 'Emerald Isle'. Shades of green were all around. Sea green, emerald green, booger green, pale green and even some shades of green that Finn was pretty sure didn't exist anywhere else. Granda would say, "Ah, the good Lord must really love the colour green, seein' as how He made so much of it!"

"Still," thought Finn, "Granda says a lot of funny things!"

He loved how his Granda spoke in his thick Irish accent. He loved his stories and the way he described things. He would say things like, "There's never a door closed till there's another one shut!" or "Rome wasn't burnt in a day!" Granda always made them laugh and Finn couldn't wait to see him again.

The motorway soon turned into small winding roads lined with tall, green hedges or rough, grey stone walls. They drove through little villages with streets decorated with pubs and teashops. White cottages with red doors, stables, green post-boxes and road signs written in Irish and English whizzed by as the family got closer to Granda's house.

It seemed to take forever, but at last Finn could see the patch of the greenest grass where he and Evie would play, and the small white house with the black door and its shiny brass fiddle doorknocker and number 9.

Granda's house was upside down. The living room and small kitchen were upstairs, and you could look right out the window into the trees and watch the birds sing and play in the branches.

The three bedrooms were downstairs. Finn remembered every detail from their last visit. Mum and Dad had the room with the red door. The green door led to Granda and Gran's room, and behind the pink door was a little room for Finn and his wee sister. Last time they were there, Evie was in a cot in their parents' room but Gran had told Finn on the telephone that they now had a special room set up so the children could share. There would be a superhero cover on one of the beds and a princess on the other. Finn knew what was coming. Granda teased them, saying Finn would have the princess bed and Evie would have Spider-Man! Evie usually wanted exactly what her big brother had, but Finn knew she was fierce when it came to the colour pink. The moment she saw the beds, she'd claim the princess as her own by jumping on it and bouncing up and down until the springs squeaked.

When the car finally stopped outside the house, Finn ran straight to the door where he saw a sign written in green ink that said, *It's Yerself! Come on in!*

Finn pushed the door open and ran up the wooden stairs to the living room. The smell of freshly baked soda bread filled the house and music was coming from an old-fashioned cassette tape player in the kitchen. Granda was looking at the old pocket watch he kept in his waistcoat. (He swore that he had won the watch in an arm-wrestling contest with a little man called 'Big Fergus'.) There he was, just like Finn always remembered him: flat tweed cap, an old rag tied around his neck, a collarless shirt with the sleeves rolled up, a black woollen waistcoat that looked as if it used to belong to a suit, and black trousers that also looked like they once belonged to a suit, but not the same suit. He always wore big brown boots, even in the summer and, no matter how often he shaved, he always had spiky red and grey whiskers sprouting from his chin.

Finn loved how any word beginning with a 'T' sounded like a 'D' when Granda said it.

"Where have they got to?" he muttered (although it sounded like, 'Whirr have dey got to?'). "They are always late! They always keep me waitin' . . ."

He stopped, mid-sentence, and looked Finn straight in the eye. A look of confusion came over him. Finn had seen it before. In fact, he had seen it every time they arrived at Granda's house. The old man rubbed his chin and said, "Now, who would you be young fella? I don't recognise you at all!"

Finn laughed, "It's me, Granda . . . it's Finn!"

The old man rubbed his chin harder and looked even more confused.

"Finn who? The only Finn I know is my grandson and you can't be him. You must be twenty-eight years old!" Finn had just turned seven, but he laughed as his grandfather continued, "Sure now, Finn is just a wee baby!" Granda's face changed from confusion to a big grinning smile. The lines on his face crinkled and his eyes narrowed and sparkled. Finn always thought that even though his Granda was old, he still looked like a little boy when he smiled.

"Sure, it's yerself. My favourite Finn! My wee darlin'! And where is that sister of yours? Did you leave her in Scotland? She's a menace y'know!" Finn laughed as Granda hugged him with the kind of hug that only Grandas give – the ones that are so tight, you feel like nothing could ever hurt you. Finn liked Granda hugs.

A babyish cry of, "POPPY POP!" made Granda's eyes twinkle even more as Evie and her crazy hair burst into the room for her hug (she was not going to allow Finn to get anything that she didn't).

Granda laughed in his high-pitched giggle, and said that his arms were long enough for both of them and maybe even another one as he winked at his daughter. Finn's mum shook her head, smiled and kissed him on the cheek while Dad carried the cases in from the car.

Soon the kettle was whistling from the top of the metal plate hanging over the turf fire. Gran brought hot soda bread, cake, scones, butter, jam and a pot of thick cream to the big wooden dining table. Gran was tall and slim, with red hair that she said she 'borrowed' from a bottle. She made the best food in the world and always made sure that she had a rainbow-coloured lollipop for Evie and Finn after meals. It didn't take long for the table of food to become a table of crumbs and stains. Finn liked that his Granda and Gran never fussed about a mess at the table. It was decorated with pen marks and scratches from years gone by. Gran would say things like, "A table full of crumbs means a belly full of goodness!" Granda would agree, "Aye and, sure, the crumbs are the food that we prepare for the birds!" They always had something to say about everything, and Finn loved every word.

"Now, I wonder, have the little people left anything for you two?" Evie's eyes got as big as one of Gran's dinner plates.

She started squealing, "POPPY POP! POPPY POP!" which is the way she responded to almost everything that Granda said. Evie jumped off her chair, threw her head back and thrust both arms in the air, letting Gran know that she was ready to go to the Plum Tree in the garden. The Plum Tree was no ordinary tree. At the bottom of the tree was a tiny garden of pebbles and shells. A small knotty wooden door with brass hinges and a big wooden latch was fixed to the tree and, to the left of it, a tiny green post box, whilst, on the right, there was an equally tiny green phone box. Granda said he installed the post box and phone box for the little people who lived in the Plum Tree in case they ever needed to get a hold of him in a hurry.

As always, little packages were hanging from the branches addressed to Finn and Evie. It was the same every morning at Granda's house. He said that the little people loved giving gifts to good children. Finn got a wooden yo-yo with a Celtic pattern printed on one side and Evie got bubbles that made her very excited – again! The little people always left a note that was handwritten in the tiniest writing. It said,

Finn and Evie, welcome back to Ireland! As usual, you won't get to see us because we are awake when you are asleep but we are very glad that you are here because it makes your Granda and Gran very happy and they are always kind and help us. Have lots of fun and be careful.

Blessings upon you both

Love from
The Plum Tree Wee People.

The sun was beginning to head to bed for the night and Finn knew his mum would soon be fussing about them getting some sleep. Being with Granda was always busy. Beaches and forests, ice cream and candyfloss, movies, stories, tickles and giggles all lay ahead in the coming days. That was the 'usual stuff' at Gran and Granda's house, but Finn could never have imagined what other strange and unusual adventures might be in store on this trip.

Chapter Three

# Banshee Screams and Ice Creams

The smell of hot soda bread dripping with melted butter, bacon, sausages, eggs and pancakes filled the air. The table was laden with tangy orange juice, jugs of cream and milk and cups of steaming tea. Breakfast at Granda's house was like no other. After every meal Granda would always say, "Will that do ye 'till ye get somethin' to eat?" It made Finn smile every single time.

Soon they were at the beach. A big red tartan blanket was unfurled onto the fine white sand and picnic baskets revealed their treasures of sandwiches, scones and cake. Everyone was wearing swimsuits and beach clothes, except Granda, who wore exactly what he always wore. Once, when Finn had asked him if he was getting ready for the beach, Granda had smiled and replied, "Finn, I am ready for everything!"

The Courtown Beach was small but perfect. You could dig in the sand, swim in the water and play on the beach for hours. The sun was warm, but the Irish Sea was always icy cold and when Finn started to shiver and his lips turned blue, Granda enfolded him in a huge towel and rubbed him up and down so hard that his feet left the floor. After a while, Evie grew tired and snuggled up to Gran for a nap. "C'mon young fella," winked Granda to Finn. "Let's go for a wander in the wild woods."

The pair headed off into the forest that skirted the coastline. Finn knew there would be stories in store. Granda was a master storyteller and Finn loved to hear all about the myths and legends and magical creatures of The Emerald Isle. The woods were beautiful today. Sunbeams filtered through the magnificent oaks, making the brilliant green foliage sparkle with what looked like fairy dust; the rustle of busy animals kept them on guard for mysterious creatures that lurked and stalked as they walked the ancient land.

"Can I tell you a story, Granda?" Finn said as they reached a clearing and perched on a twisted tree trunk to rest a while.

"Just like your Old Granda does, eh? You get to be like the people you are with, y'know," Granda said, smiling down at him. "Sure, that would be just brilliant!"

Finn's arms began to wave as he relayed the story of the journey from Scotland to Ireland. He described the big boat in every detail from the kids' play area, right through to the big rivets that held the ship together. Granda listened and nodded and thought to himself,

"The lad has the gift of the gab, for sure. No need for this one to kiss that old stone at Blarney."

Finn continued his yarn, and, like any good storyteller, he built up the excitement and tension as he reached the best part – the strange thing that had happened in the car just before they had driven off the boat. He took Granda's hands and looked him straight in the eye and whispered, "Then the music changed from fast and furious fiddles to a low moan. It looked like it was coming from Mum and as she slowly turned, the face I saw was not the face of my mum." Finn paused for dramatic effect, keeping his eyes fixed on his Granda. "The face was scary and beautiful at the same time. Dark, dark eyes and red, red lips, but the scariest thing was the sound she made. First a low moan, then a cry, then a SCREAM!" Granda let go of Finn's hands and covered his mouth. He turned a little pale and his eyes were wide and glaring.

"Did the woman say anything to you, Finn?"

"It was just a dream, Granda!" Finn laughed, delighted at his Granda's response. "I woke up when Dad bumped the car onto the big ramp."

"Aye, but this is very important now, Finn," said Granda sternly. "Did the woman say anything to you?"

"Nope, she just screamed."

Granda took Finn by the hand again and said, "Let's go get some ice cream."

Finn didn't think any more about the strange woman. He liked the feeling that he'd impressed his Granda with his story, but now he was focused on just one thing. The pair set off at a pace, back towards the beach and the little shack that sold the best ice cream in the whole of Ireland.

Finn sat on the big blanket watching his little sister drop her ice cream cone in the sand and then eat it anyway. He could hear Granda whispering to his mum. Mum was shaking her head as Granda kept saying, "But you need to be sure . . . you need to be sure . . ." Mum shook her head and kissed him on the cheek.

"Dad, he's too young. Don't go filling his head with your stories."

"Well now, there are some stories that we need to hear . . . and we need to be sure!" Mum smiled and kissed him again and muttered something under her breath.

After more swimming and digging and lots of squealing from Evie, the family packed up the car and headed back to the house.

Soon it was time for hot showers, warm pyjamas and something else to eat before bedtime. Evie was already snoring on the couch. Dad picked her up and tucked her into her bed. Granda walked downstairs with Finn and threw the big colourful superhero duvet right over him so it covered Finn's head. They played a 'Peek-a-Boo' game for a few minutes. Sometimes Granda treated him like he was still just a baby, but Finn didn't mind. He knew how much his Granda loved him. The old fella reached out his right hand and placed it on his grandson's head. Looking at the boy, he said in a hushed voice, "Now, you sleep well, and dream only good dreams." Finn couldn't help feeling that his Granda looked concerned about something,

"What is it Granda? What's wrong?"

"Och, it's no time to talk now. You have some sleeping to do!"

With that, he kissed him on the forehead and went back upstairs. Finn waited until Granda left the room before he put his thumb in his mouth and sucked it until he fell asleep.

Finn woke early to the sound of pots and pans clanging in the kitchen. He opened his eyes to see his little sister standing beside his bed just staring at him. She stared well. Finn thought that if staring was an Olympic sport, Evie would win the Gold Medal. He climbed out of bed and headed upstairs while Evie just stood there holding her baby doll by the neck, her wild red hair tangled in sleep knots, staring and sucking a big purple dummy. She made no sound, except for one quacking noise that Finn was pretty sure didn't come from her mouth.

As usual, the breakfast table was fit to burst with good things and Gran swept by carrying a big jug of milk, ruffled Finn's hair with her free hand and said, "Mornin' young fella."

"What's the plan, Granda?" asked Finn.

"How about a movie over at Gorey Cinema? It's Kids' Club at ten o'clock."

It was agreed. They would head over to the cinema mid-morning, so for now Mum busied herself on her phone, posting messages and pictures of their day at the beach, while Gran began putting out bright coloured paints and big white sheets of paper for her and Evie to make pictures.

Finn looked over at Dad, who was already snoring in the big red armchair. He never understood how his Dad could sleep so much when they were holiday!

Granda winked at Finn and picked up the stick he liked to take when he went for his morning walk (he called it his Blackthorn Shillelagh).[2] Finn didn't even need to ask if he could come too. He just looked at his Granda and the old fella smiled and nodded. Finn liked the way he and his Granda could speak to each other without saying a word. It was like magic.

The two of them walked down by the old harbour, their footsteps and click of the walking stick echoing off the ancient stone walls.

"Why do you carry a walking stick when you don't even have a limp, Granda?"

He answered in his thickest, strongest, posh Irish accent.

"Well now lad, an Irish gentleman should always have his Shillelagh in his hand when he is walking. Sometimes it is important that he knows how to behave in a way that some people might think is not very gentlemanly!" Finn scratched his head and screwed up his nose. This sounded like another of

2. Shillelagh, pronounced 'Shil-lay-lay' – A walking stick.

his Granda's riddles. "How can a gentleman not behave gentlemanly?' he asked. The old man's eyes twinkled as he replied, "Not everything is what it seems, Finny boy!"

As they neared the ice cream booth by the harbour, the owner raised his hand in a wave. Shea was a jolly man, as round as he was high. He clearly liked to sample plenty of his own ice cream. He wore a large floppy white hat and a big white double-breasted jacket that was stained with red dots. By the time they reached the booth, Shea had whipped up two large vanilla cones dripping with strawberry syrup. Finn mentioned that his mum said that ice cream was not breakfast food, but Shea insisted that was not a rule, rather a suggestion.

On the way back home, Granda began to hum a tune that eventually turned into a song. It sounded like some old dirge that had been around forever.

*"Sure the land that we are living in*
*'Tis glorious to behold*
*It is green and it is lovely*
*It has hidden pots of gold.*
*There is much our eyes can follow*
*There is much we can perceive*
*But there's even more to know*
*Through the eyes that can believe."*

Finn smiled and slipped his sticky hand into his Granda's as the song continued and they walked to its rhythm.

*"Oh among the trees and wildflowers*
*Other eyes are looking back*
*Other voices that are whispering*
*As we wander down each track.*
*There are blessings that are hidden*
*There are things that make you grieve*
*Ahh, but you can only see them*
*Through the eyes that can believe."*

Finn listened carefully to the words, thinking that his Granda had a pretty good singing voice.

"Do you think that's true, Granda? Do you think there are things that we can't see?"

The old man stopped walking and looked at the boy. He stooped low until he and Finn were face to face. "Now, I didn't say that we couldn't see them. I said that we could see them . . . if we believe! For instance, was your 'dream' about the lady with the dark, dark eyes and the red, red lips just a dream or were you looking through believing eyes? Be sure of this, young Finny . . . not everything is what it seems."

"Och Granda, everybody would think I was mad if I thought it was true! I mean, how could she even get in the car?" Finn laughed, giving his Granda a small punch in the arm.

"Well now Finny boy, only someone who has been 'touched in the head' would say such taradiddle, but if you know and trust the person who says it, then maybe it's true, otherwise why else would you say it?"

"But it had to be a dream, right?"

Granda looked very seriously at Finn. He looked around as if he was checking to see that no one was watching, stooped low again and whispered, "Tell me, young fella, this woman with the dark, dark eyes and the red, red lips, was her hair thick and white?" Finn nodded. "Was she beautiful and terrible all at the same time and did you feel her scream more than you could hear it?" Finn's eyes widened as he nodded again. "Was she wearing a white dress and did her hair and clothing look as if they were being blown by a strong wind?" Finn could barely manage to get the word out but a small cracked "yes" dropped off his lips. "Granda . . . how did you know?"

"I know because I have seen her too," Granda replied, his voice low and unusually serious. "She is our Banshee[3] and she only comes for one reason."

The boy's eyes widened further. He knew the old tales of the Irish Banshees. Granda had spun these yarns before,

3. Banshee, pronounced 'Ban-she' – A female spirit.

how they moaned and screamed . . . how they came to warn of a death. Suddenly Finn felt very afraid.

"Granda! If it was Banshee that's bad, right? They only come for one reason, right? She comes to let you know that . . ."

"Try not to fret, young fella. You would be right to be concerned, but remember Finn, not everything is as it seems."

The two continued the walk back home with Granda picking up his Irish tune. Finn was no longer listening, though. He couldn't help wondering why a Banshee would come to him. He also wondered what 'taradiddle' meant.

Chapter Four

# Somebody's Watching

The movie was fun and the candy was good. In the afternoon, they visited a small farm called 'Kia-Ora'. The children got to hold baby animals and drive mechanical diggers made just for kids, although Granda and Dad seemed to enjoy them as well. By teatime, everyone was feeling tired enough to agree that a night by the fire sounded like a grand idea. The following day Mum and Dad were set to leave on a kid-free five-day break to Dublin. Finn thought it sounded very boring and was glad he and Evie would get to stay at Granda's house instead. Imagine Dublin with no kids! Mum seemed pretty excited though, and kept doing that corny 'mum dance', as she told the children how much she loved them and how much she'd miss them. Finn and Evie didn't mind being left with Granda and Gran one bit. Who else gives you ice cream for breakfast?

Mum and Dad packed the car in super-fast time and Mum gave Granda and Gran a list of things to remember.

"Here's our mobile phone number. This one is mine, that one is Paul's. You can also FaceTime us or use any App that allows video calls. Here's the name, actual address, email address and phone number of the hotel we are staying at. They have someone on the desk twenty-four seven. Call if you need us, or if you need to tell us anything, or if something happens, but make sure you call us, because if we don't hear from you we will start thinking something is wrong."

Finn smiled to himself knowingly as he watched Granda nodding but clearly not paying any attention whatsoever as Mum prattled on and on and on. Granda and Gran didn't care much for mobile phones or computers. He would say, "I don't need to be on 'Face Cloth' or 'The Inter Webs' or whatever it is you young 'uns call that virtual world. I would rather be connected to what's around me in the real world than live in a 'virtual world' where you learn 'virtually nuthin'." He wasn't a fan.

Dad bundled Mum – still giving her parents lists of instructions – into the car. She fastened her seatbelt as Dad turned the ignition key and the engine coughed into life. Mum was still shouting directives as they drove off, mingled with "Love you . . . we will miss you . . . byeee!"

As the car disappeared around the corner, they all went back into the house and sat in the quietness left by Mum's absent voice. It didn't last long.

"POPPY POP! POPPY POP!" Yes, Evie was ready to roll and everybody had to know about it.

"I think we may need to tire that one out," said Granda. Gran and Finn nodded in agreement and they decided to head off for a long walk in the woods. The woods seemed even more magical today. Slices of sunlight squeezed through every gap in the trees, branches and leaves. It made the forest alive with colour. Every shade of green, of course, but yellows and deep reds all blended together like the paints on an artist's palette, one colour running into the other and creating something new. The forest floor was a collage of brown and red dirt mixed with white sand that had blown up from the beach, the odd muddy patch and an occasional animal poo. Small birds fluttered from tree to tree and Finn looked up to see the occasional magpie staring at the travellers as they marched by.

It was a perfect place for a game of hide and seek. Evie toddled through the undergrowth and they all acted surprised when she hid behind a tree then jumped out at them. Gran was a great actress, but Finn thought she overdid it a bit. Still, her startled response got Evie squealing and in fits of infectious giggles.

The woods were wonderfully alive with colour and laughter and creatures making their homes . . . but in the darker parts of the forest, down deep in the tangled weeds and long grass, other eyes were watching . . . green eyes that glowed in the shadows.

The walk back home had a short detour past Shea's Ice Cream Booth where Granda bought four gigantic cones, bigger than Evie's head. By the time they were home, Evie's whole face was white and red with ice cream and raspberry sauce stains and Finn licked at his ice cream moustache knowing that his Gran would be at him with the facecloth if he didn't remove every remnant.

While Gran scrubbed Evie, Finn got ready for bed and Granda prepared some teacakes and hot chocolate with marshmallows for supper. It wasn't long until Evie was snoring and Finn could feel his eyelids getting heavy as he drifted off to the land of nod. Very soon, the lights were switched off and there were no sounds in the house except for those of contented sleepers. Meanwhile, outside, the grass made some rustling sounds as if the wind was blowing through it. But there was no wind this night, not even a breeze. Yet there it was again, as quiet as a church mouse wearing slippers, just the smallest rustle and then . . . three pairs of green luminous eyes, peering through the bedroom window at two children sleeping in their beds.

Chapter Five

# The Times They Are a Changeling

Finn loved the first stretch of the morning – the one that makes some of your bones click and, together with a big loud yawn, lets your whole body know that it has rested enough and it's time to get up and start the day.

Finn opened his eyes to the sight of Evie's crazy red hair close to his face. It made him jump. She stood there, dummy in her mouth, hugging her baby doll and calling Finn by name, repeating it over and over. That was different. She usually called him 'KEE KEE'. He threw off his Spider-Man duvet and kissed Evie on the head. She looked up at him and giggled. Finn didn't notice the touch of green light in her eyes as they both raced upstairs for breakfast.

As usual, the table was full of food: toasted soda bread with melted butter, pancakes and syrup, orange juice and tea, cream, milk, sausages, bacon, toast and eggs with mushrooms and tomatoes. Gran had prepared most of it before she left for market and Granda was smiling and rubbing his hands as the children ran to the table.

"Will this do for now?" he said.

"At least until we get something to eat!" yelled Finn. They all laughed and began to attack the food on the table. Finn had the same as Granda – a large plate of eggs and bacon with soda bread and a big glass of orange juice. Evie had the same. Granda washed it all down with tea from a big mug that had 'World's Best Grandad' printed on one side. Finn had bought it for him out of his own pocket money and Granda said that it was his favourite mug. Evie had the same, which seemed a little strange since she had never drunk tea before. Then she ate the rest of the pancakes, the syrup and all of the soda bread. She drank the milk, the orange juice and ate the rest of the bacon and eggs. Then she licked the plate and grabbed the last sausage and gnawed into that as well. Granda and Finn sat silently and watched until the old fella said, "Is she always this hungry?' Finn shook his head as they watched her drain the last of the cream from the jug and then eat the jam, straight from the pot.

"Now that is probably enough for darlin'," Granda smiled as he reached over to wipe Evie's mouth. Without warning, she snarled and snapped at his fingers with what looked like sharp little fangs. Her eyes glowed green and even though it looked like Evie, she was behaving weirder than usual!

Granda leapt out of his chair and put himself between Finn and his little sister.

"What is it Granda? What's wrong with Evie?" asked Finn in alarm.

"Finn, I need you to do what I tell you. Trust me, that is not your sister!"

Finn peeked around Granda's waistcoat to see Evie standing on her chair, covered in jam, egg and syrup stains and staring at Granda with strange green eyes!

"Finn I need you to go over to the hearth and hand me the iron shovel." At that point, the old man started singing the song that Finn had heard the day before. Finn quietly walked across the room, lifted the old black shovel and went back behind his Granda. Still singing, the old man backed himself and his grandson into the kitchen. Evie's green eyes never once stopped looking at the old man's face. It was as if the song had enchanted her. Once in the kitchen, Granda lifted the old heavy iron frying pan and made his way back to Evie.

"Now little one, what business do you have here in my house? Your kind should know better than to come to my home. But, more importantly, where is my granddaughter?" Finn peeked out once again to see his sister's face change from the happy little red-headed girl to a grinning impish creature who spoke with a scratchy voice,

"Oh, we took her. She is beautiful. We need a new queen. Only a beautiful queen will do and she will make a beautiful queen . . . in another sixteen of your years!"

"Is that so, Changeling?[4] Well, we will need to see about that!" Quick as a flash, Granda pulled

4. Changeling, pronounced 'Change-ling' – A fairy who changes places with a human.

the iron shovel from Finn's hand and swung it at the creature, knocking it off the chair. It crashed hard against the wall but instantly jumped to its bony little feet and hissed as it lunged back at Granda. Finn watched, frozen to the spot as the creature moved faster than any human, springing around the dining room in a green whirl. Even more amazing, though, was Granda as he countered every move and attack with his household weapons. Finn gazed, open mouthed, as the Changeling bit down hard on the shovel with its sharp teeth. It lashed out at Granda but the old man blocked its jaggy little nails with the frying pan. Then, when it tried to leap or jump at Finn, the old fella blocked or counter attacked with his makeshift sword and shield.

After lots of jumping and swinging, biting and scratching – as well as lots of whacks with the pan and shovel – the creature began to move more slowly. Sensing its weariness, Granda moved like lightning and sandwiched it between the pan and the shovel, where it gave a hideous scream and rather unpleasantly seemed to break wind. As it writhed and squirmed, Finn couldn't help noticing how strong his Granda's arms looked. He had never noticed before, but the old man could move faster than any person he had ever seen and, even though he wasn't a big man, Finn could see that he was super strong.

"Now, tell me. Where is the girl?" Granda demanded, his voice low and eerie.

The creature spat and hissed and insisted that it would never tell.

"Is that so now?" Without flinching, Granda moved towards the hearth, the creature still securely clamped between frying pan and shovel.

"It's feeling a wee bit cold in here, maybe a bit of the old fire can warm us all up?" Granda grinned at the creature menacingly.

The little monster began to gulp. The iron was hurting enough by now, but fire? Changelings hated iron, but they feared fire. As the old man brought the pan closer to the flames it began whining and writhing even more, but Granda's strong arms kept the black metal shovel hard against its chest, pinning it to the pan.

"Warm enough for you there?" Granda smiled through gritted teeth as he spoke, making the creature yelp even more. Little beads of sweat began to run down its leathery skin as it screamed, "You wouldn't dare! You wouldn't dare hurt a fairy creature! You know what we can do to you and your family! YOU WOULDN'T DARE!"

"Ahh, now sure I'm not the brightest man in Ireland. Dim as a winter's evening in Wexford I am. What I don't know would fill a barn, but be sure of this, Changeling, I *do know* you and your kind, and I know that you know me too. So, it would seem to me that you shouldn't dare me because I think you know how I respond to threats!" The little beast's eyes widened, and a red tongue flicked in and out of its lipless mouth as the pan got closer still to the fire.

"They have taken her to Tara! Tara, that's where you will find her!"

Removing the pan from the fire, the old man walked to the door with the Changeling. He looked deep into its glowing eyes and cocked his head a little to the left. After a long few seconds of silence he moved his face within inches of the creature and said in a low menacing voice, "You tell your scrawny little 'king' that he has made a big mistake! If my granddaughter isn't back here by noon, tell him that I will come and get her myself and he will not like that! You do understand this message don't you, ya wee eejit?"[5] The Changeling nodded its sweaty head and before it could utter another word Granda said, "Now go, tell him!" and he tossed the fairy high into the air in the same way that he would flip a pancake. With a great *THWACKING* sound, he slapped it so hard with the shovel that the little creature flew high over the trees into the woods. Granda took his pocketwatch out of his waistcoat. It was 11:15 am. He looked at Finn and said, "This is not good. Finn, I may need your help!"

5. Eejit, pronounced 'E-jit' – An idiot.

Chapter Six

# A Brief History of Finn

Granda began to throw various items into an old brown canvas backpack while Finn tried to work out what had just happened. He had lots of, 'What, why and how' questions for Granda, who said that he would answer everything in the car but right now, time was running out. The backpack was filled with a box of salt and some rope, an old book of poems and songs, the iron poker from the hearth set, some sweets, apples, an old tennis ball, some things that Finn had never seen before and a bottle of something that looked like it might make you very drunk. Granda checked his watch again. It was five minutes to midday. The old man's eyebrows seemed to drop right down to his eyeballs as he looked at his grandson, "You will be needing a warm coat and some boots, Finny boy . . . now!"

Finn had never seen this look on the old man's face before. It was determined, thoughtful and a little bit menacing.

Finn put on his boots and pulled a warm, waterproof hooded jacket over his head. Granda looked at his watch again. This was unusual. Finn knew his Granda treasured that watch, but he never much cared about the time. He often said, "God made time, but man made haste." Now they both seemed to be holding their breath as they watched both hands on the watch standing erect at the XII position waiting for the second hand to catch up.

*Tick, tick, tick, tick . . .* Noon.

"Right, we've waited long enough," said Granda, with a determined sigh.

Granda pushed his cap back and looked at the front door as if expecting someone to walk through it. There was silence. He waited only ten seconds before picking up a pen and scribbling a note for Gran that read:

> Changelings swapped Evie . . . I could be a while. The boy is with me. It is time for him to know. We need to go to Tara . . . you know what this means.
>
> Love
>
> S
>
> P.S. We are out of jam.

The old man grabbed his Blackthorn Shillelagh, pulled on a black jacket that looked as if it used to belong to a suit (but not the same suit as the waistcoat or trousers), pulled his cap down hard and said, "Right boyo, we need to go!"

"Go? Go where?"

"Go and bring your wee sister home!"

The pair climbed into the old, rusty, sky-blue Volkswagen Beetle when Finn said, "Shouldn't we phone Mum?"

"Och," sighed the old fella. "Sure she'd just yell at me and tell me to go and do what we are about to go and do anyway!"

The car kicked into life as Granda crunched the gears into place and muttered something under his breath as the car bounced over the dirty, bumpy country roads. Finn couldn't hold on any longer. The questions came shooting out of him faster than a fat lady on a water slide. "What was that? What happened to my sister? What made her change? And how did you move like that? What kind of Granda are you?"

"That wasn't your sister, Finn. That was a Changeling – nasty wee fairy folk who steal into children's rooms when they are asleep and swap them for one of their own. They have the power to look like the child they took, but they can't help being what they are. Greedy, nasty, angry wee hallions, every one of them.[6] You can't trust them and they will eat you out of house and home! They take children for all kinds of reasons and it seems they are wanting a new queen. We need to bring Evie back home."

Finn heard "WHAT?" in his brain, but he couldn't get the word to drop the five inches to his mouth.

6. Hallion, pronounced 'Hal-yon' – A contemptible person.

The old man took a deep breath and began to speak very gently.

"Now listen, Finny boy, because this is going to sound like the ranting of a madman, but believe me, every single word is true."

Finn got that feeling that you get when you need to swallow but you have no spit to do it. The old fella continued, "There are some things that you need to know about your old Granda and our family. It is true that no family is ever just ordinary, but our family are particularly extraordinary." Finn felt his eyes widen.

"We are from a particular blood line here in Ireland. Our history is more than interesting; it's magical! Our great, great, great, great, great . . . och, too many 'greats' to remember! The thing is, we come from a very important family that makes us very special."

Finn looked confused. He wasn't special at all. He was just a normal seven-year-old boy who liked to play video games and loved Spider-Man. He was a bit taller than most boys his age. He had freckles around his nose and cheeks and had one bit of hair at the back of his head that always stood up. He liked ice cream and puddings and he was an average student at school, except for art and writing stories. He was excellent at these things! Then he thought about what he had just seen his old Granda do back at the house. He sat quietly and listened.

"Does the name Fionn MacCumhaill mean anything to you?"[7]

7. Fionn MacCumhaill, pronounced 'Finn Ma-cool' – A famous Irish hero.

Finn shook his head.

"Well now, a long time ago in Ireland there was a great hero called Fionn MacCumhaill, but you might remember him from the bedtime and hearth time stories I have told you. Finn McCool?"

Finn smiled as he remembered the stories about giants and causeways, spitting contests and monsters.

"Oh yeah, Granda, I love those fairy tales!"

The old man turned and smiled as he whispered, "Ahh, but you see, Finny boy, they aren't fairy stories! Do you think that we called you 'Finn' by accident?"

Finn had only ever thought about why he was called 'Finn' once in his whole life. In his head, he decided it must be because his mum liked sharks.

Granda carried on. "Our family are the descendants of Finn McCool himself. That means we have some very special gifts. Your old Granda inherited, hmm . . . how can we say it? Well, let's say that I have a few special quirks that come in very handy sometimes. The gifts vary in each generation, but once in a while one is born who will be more like our ancient grandfather Finn McCool, more than others have in previous generations. So, when you told me about our Banshee paying you a wee visit, it got me thinking. Finn, your old Granda thinks that there are great things in store for you!"

"But Granda, if the Banshee comes, doesn't that mean that . . . that . . . that . . ."

"That death is coming? Yes it does, Finn! Isn't that marvellous? The Banshee never visits anyone when they are seven years old. It's usually old people who get that privilege."

"I don't like the Banshee," Finn protested, wondering why his Granda could possibly think this death messenger was marvellous news. "I don't want to see her ever again, Granda!"

The old man smiled and put his hand on Finn's head. "I know, I know. But remember, Finn. Not everything is what it seems!"

Finn wished that Granda would stop saying that. They drove for a long time until they hit thick dark woodland where Granda stopped the car.

"We need to go on foot from here boyo, and try not to worry. I will take care of you, but I will need your help to get Evie back. Can I count on you to be brave?"

Finn looked up at his grandfather and nodded but, in truth, he did not feel very brave at all. Scared, terrified, petrified, panicking, or even 'pooing yourself', seemed much better words to describe how he really felt. The old man ruffled his hair with one hand as he threw the old backpack over his shoulder and picked up his walking stick with the other. "Right then. Let's do this," he said, with a look of determination and a twinkle in his eye.

Granda and Finn set out into the trees, stomping deeper into the woods, unaware that a pair of red eyes was watching them from the long grass, far behind the thick oak trees.

Chapter Seven

# The Black Dog

They seemed to walk for hours in the woods. Even though they had arrived in the afternoon, the thick green foliage made the forest dim and dull. Whatever daylight was left was going fast and Finn was feeling tired and hungry. The old man just kept going with strong and steady strides but, when he finally noticed that Finn was falling behind, he drew to a halt.

"OK, Finny boy, let's sit for a moment and have something to eat."

He pulled two big shiny red apples from his backpack. They sat on a large black rock and Finn took a bite. The apple was crunchy and so juicy that some of it dribbled down his chin. He giggled and looked up at Granda but, to his horror, a pair of bright red eyes was looking down on them both from behind the old man. Finn dropped his apple and pointed a shaky finger. He tried to find the words, but the words wouldn't come. Granda watched as Finn raised his finger and pointed to something behind him. Something that was big and breathing icy blasts down his neck.

As Granda spun around, the creature let out three long spine-tingling howls then became silent once again as it bared long white fangs, covered in dripping glistening slobbers that dangled like the slimy stuff your nose makes on very cold days.

Granda only had the time to gasp, "Cu Sidhe!" as the beast lunged at him.[8] It looked like a dog but it was as big as a bull with thick black shining hair and scars all over its powerful body. The beast's jaws snapped as Granda leapt back and put himself between the sharp teeth and his grandson. The great dog paced back and forth, never taking its red eyes off its prey. The only sound Finn could hear was that of his own heart beating and the monstrous paws crunching twigs and pebbles as it moved across the forest floor.

Snatching the box of salt from his backpack, Granda poured some into his right hand and made a fist as he said, "Cu Sidhe! Are your masters sending a dog to do a man's work?"

The dog's lips pulled back tighter as if it understood the insult. It lunged once again and the massive jaws opened wide as Granda flung his fist forward, letting the handful of salt fly down the dog's throat and all over its red tongue. The creature stopped in its tracks. Its face contorted as its whole body began to shake and shudder. Then, suddenly, it fell over on one side and lay motionless. Finn was almost frozen in fear.

"Is it dead? What is it anyway?" he managed to stammer, after what seemed like a very long time.

8. Cu Sidhe, pronounced 'Coo-She' – A fairy hound.

Granda whispered, "It's a Cu Sidhe, a fairy hound. They are sent to do the dirty work of them wee hallions. The black dog is merciless and can torment anyone if it gets the chance, but no, he's not dead, only an angel blade will do that job. The salt will make him dopey for a minute or two, so we need to move . . . now!"

Granda grabbed Finn by the hand and ran. Sometimes Finn felt as if his feet were leaving the ground as Granda pulled him forward. He could run much faster than other Grandas . . . much, much faster. Suddenly Finn felt his hand being yanked away as something huge slammed into the old man. The fairy hound was back and seemed angrier than ever. Granda took the brunt of the impact as the dog's massive head slammed into his ribs. Finn rolled through the grass and stopped when he hit an old tree stump. He turned to see Granda on his back in the long grass and the hound towering over him. The beast put a huge paw on Granda's chest and some of the slimy snotty stuff from its mouth dripped onto his face. Finn was terrified that the weight of the black dog would crush the old man.

Just then, the clouds parted, and the woodland was lit by a full moon. The hound threw its head back and howled three long and terrible cries as the silver light illuminated its black shining coat against the shadows of the forbidding forest.

The dog slowly looked down from the moon to the face of the old man pinned below. It seemed to smile for a moment before it opened its hideous jaws wide and with a sense of delight, lowered them towards the old man's neck. Finn watched in horror as he saw Granda push his hands into the grass, twisting it and wrapping it around his fingers. The dog's fangs were inches from his neck when suddenly Granda ripped the long grass from the ground and punched the beast with a mossy green fist. The creature let out a yelp of agony. In that split second, Granda jumped to his feet and began to dance, bob and sway more gracefully than a professional boxer. "C'mon . . . is that the best you can do, big lad?" he taunted. The hound shook its head, then turned and attacked once again, but Granda was faster than the beast now. He landed another two punches on the beast's right eye and ribs. Small trickles of dark red blood began to run down the hound's face as it turned and attacked again. The old man stood firm and, with a strong left hook and an upper cut, the dog was lifted off its four big paws and knocked squarely onto its backside. It whimpered and got back on all fours, but it didn't look quite so confident as it ran again one final time towards Granda. With perfect timing, the old man drew back his right arm and, as the dog came into reach, two grassy fists began to repeatedly hit the monster's head like a gym punch ball. Soon the great beast was whimpering like a puppy as it turned and ran with its hairy tail firmly between its hairy legs.

Granda shouted, "Aye, let that be a lesson to you. And tell your masters I will see them soon enough!"

Finn and Granda sat in silence for a few moments, catching their breath. Finn could hardly believe that the man who had just beaten a fearsome fairy hound in a fight was his old Granda.

"Granda! How? I mean, what? I mean, didn't you say that only an 'angel's blade' could really stop the black fairy hound? How did you do that?"

The old man took a deep breath, removed his grassy boxing gloves and brushed the dirt off his jacket.

"Did you notice that old book of poetry and songs I always carry with me?" he said. Finn nodded.

"Well it is old wisdom, and at one time it was required of those who take the good of this world seriously that we learn it by heart. Old wisdom can save your life. Did you know that old wisdom tells us 'every blade of grass has an angel bending over it whispering "grow, grow"'?"

Finn's eyes widened as he found himself saying, "Angel's blades . . . grass!" Ireland was covered in the stuff.

The old man smiled, "You will find that most everything you need is closer than you think! Remember, Finn, not everything is as it seems." Finn looked up at his Granda. He didn't know what to think. "You need to read the old wisdom, boyo," said Granda, pulling him to his feet. "It was right then. It is right now. You will need to know it. We all need to know it, but aye, you especially are going to need to know it! Read the old book, Finny boy, read it and pay heed to it."

Barely visible through the branches and trees stood a woman dressed in white with dark, dark eyes and red, red lips. She watched for a while then vanished as she made a low mournful moan. It was hardly audible. Still, Finn felt it and shuddered as he and his Granda continued on their quest.

## Chapter Eight

# Sealed with a Kiss

The forest was now cloaked in darkness, so dark that the travellers could barely see the trees in front of them. It was getting colder too, and strange noises made them both a little twitchy. With his senses heightened, Finn thought he could hear the sound of the ocean. They walked on and, sure enough, they soon came to a clifftop with crashing waves far below. The tree line ran right along the edge of the cliff and Granda said that it was important to pay attention, or you might easily miss that first 'big step'. Finn looked out to the sea and shimmering moonlight then, just for a short moment, wished he were in his Spider-Man bed, safe and warm.

The cold was starting to bite and the fight with the Cu Sidhe had left them both exhausted. Finn was just wondering if they were going to find his sister and make it home before bedtime when he picked up another sound on the night breeze. Granda heard it too. Sweet, gentle singing drifted through the dark woods. It took a little time to discover where it was coming from, but it didn't take them long to start walking towards the tune. It was a beautiful song and it made the two travellers smile. Not far from the forest edge, they began to make out the shape of a small white cottage with thatch for a roof. A light burned in the window and they were sure the music was coming from within.

As they drew close, they could make out a woman through the window. She was preparing food in the kitchen and singing the most beautiful song with the most beautiful voice. Granda's mouth fell open and he lost the power to blink. Long, raven black hair framed a face so radiant it put the full moon in the sky to shame.

They watched in silence as she pushed her jet-black locks back from her porcelain white face and sang as she worked.

*"Come you maidens fair and young*
*listen to the song I've sung*
*its tune you'll likely hear 'less you pay heed*
*Though I live in finery*
*sure it all means naught to me*
*for I did not end up here because of greed*

*Trust not silver, trust not gold*
*they leave you empty, leave you cold*
*never trust the one who hides a sleekit grin*[9]
*he'll take everything from you*
*and you won't know what to do*
*when you're a prisoner in the skin that you are in . . ."*

9. Sleekit, pronounced 'Sle-kit' – Sly or deceitful.

Finn glanced at his Granda, who was still staring, mesmerized. The woman, blissfully unaware she was being watched, continued her song.

*"And come all you gentlemen*
*Sure I'll sing it once again*
*if you'll only act in love all would be fine*
*For true love does not possess*
*it is born in righteousness*
*and it never owns or says, 'Now you're mine!'*

*Trust not silver, trust not gold*
*they leave you empty leave you cold*
*never trust the one who hides a sleekit grin*
*he'll take everything from you*
*and you won't know what to do*
*when you're a prisoner in the skin that you are in."*

Just as she finished her sad but beautiful lament, she looked up and spied the two figures outside the window. "Who's there? Show yourselves!" she shouted.

"We don't mean to intrude but we are cold and tired, and my grandson is young and not used to the darkness of the woods."

Finn gave his Granda a dirty look as the old man winked and smiled back.

The front door made a creaking noise as it opened and the beautiful woman invited them into the house. She wore a green dress that dropped down below the knee and over it she draped a white apron.

It was warm inside and the house smelled of baked bread and turf from the fire. The woman motioned with her hand and pointed to the bench seat by the big table. The travellers sat down.

"So, what would you be doing in the woods at this time of night, sir?"

Granda rubbed his chin and replied, "Well now, it's an adventure of sorts. We are playing a big game of 'hide and seek' with the boy's sister and sure wouldn't you know it, she is *very* good at hiding!"

"In the forest?" said the woman.

"Oh aye," replied Granda.

"In the middle of the night? Tell me, how old is your sister, young lad?"

Finn wasn't sure what to say but, in the end, he knew that the truth was the best option.

"She is two and a bit," he replied. Granda pulled his cap down over his eyes and looked at the floor.

"Two and a bit. And she is hiding in the woods in the dark? Seriously?" The woman put her hands on her hips the way Gran often did when she was telling Granda off.

Granda looked up, "Well now, if you knew the whole story you'd understand, but it's a bit hard to believe."

The woman gave him a steely stare and said, "Try me!"

Just then, there were heavy footsteps and a man walked into the room. The woman fell silent and went back to chopping vegetables on the big wooden table.

He was a big man and wore a rough woollen sweater and a woollen hat. His trousers were old and stained and tucked into a pair of long rubber boots. He clenched a long pipe between his teeth and Finn thought he was probably a fisherman.

"So, who have we here, my love?' The woman didn't look at him but answered his question in a very quiet voice.

"Just two hungry travellers, lost in the woods."

The big man put his hands on her shoulders and said, "Well now, my name is Damien and I am very glad that you found us. It is going to be a miserably wet night outside and my lovely wife Farraige makes the tastiest food in the world."[10] Finn and his Granda couldn't help noticing how Farraige shrugged her husband's hands from her shoulders and went to the stove to boil the water.

In no time at all, big bowls of potato and leek soup were on the table beside plates of doorstep-thick bread for dipping. In less time still, the bowls were empty and Farraige was putting sheets on the two couches in the next room. "I am very sorry that we don't have beds for you but you will be warm and comfortable on the sofas by the fire."

Damien offered Granda a drink of a clear liquid that had a funny smell while Finn sipped on a mug

10. Farraige, pronounced 'Far-e-ga' – Beside or close to the sea.

of hot milk. The woman never spoke again until she excused herself and went to bed, while Damien sat and talked for a while. Sure enough, he was a fisherman and he and his wife had been married for just a year. He said that she was the most amazing wife. She could cook and clean, mend his clothes and make sure everything was ready for him when he returned from his boat. He seemed very happy with his wife but Finn and Granda both felt that she, on the other hand, had seemed very sad indeed.

The couch was just as comfy as any bed that Finn had slept in, but when he put his head on the pillow there was a rustling sound. Finn tried to get to sleep for a long time, but the sound was driving him crazy. He pushed his hand inside the pillow cover to see what was so noisy and pulled out a crumpled piece of paper. The words on it seemed to have been written in haste,

*"I have a house but no home,*
*A man but no husband,*
*Fine clothes but no fur,*
*Company but no community.*
*I need my coat so I can leave.*
*Help me if you understand."*

Granda was snoring on the other couch. It took a good hard shake to wake him, but Finn knew it was important to show him the note. He watched as the old man's face changed. "I knew it," he muttered.

"Get dressed, Finny boy. We have some work to do. And be quiet!" Finn pulled on his sweater and jeans and thought how funny it was that, no matter how hard you tried to be quiet in the middle of the night, you always made noises. Boots sounded louder on floorboards, doors creaked at high volume, a waterproof jacket sounded as though someone was crushing bags of 'Tayto' when you pulled it over your head![11]

Soon the two of them were in the kitchen and Granda whispered, "Now, we are looking for something very special, Finn. It will be hidden someplace in or near the house. It will look like a fur coat, but it will smell of salt and seaweed. If you find it, don't shout, just bring it to me. OK?"

Finn nodded and the pair began to look in cupboards and boxes around the little house. With every sound Finn thought they would wake the sleeping couple, but Damien's snoring and snorting echoed through the house like a rumbling volcano. It sounded like a pig hunting for truffles. After an hour or so of opening and closing a lot of drawers and cupboard doors and even looking under a few loose floorboards, there was still no sign of the fur coat. Granda waved his hand to go outside. The rain had stopped and the sun was starting to rise. Little orange shards of sunlight cut through the morning mist and made the wet trees and grass

11. Tayto, pronounced 'Tay-toe' – Irish potato crisps.

sparkle like fairy dust. Granda whispered again, "If it's not in the house it will be close by, Finn. It is a very important thing and Damien wouldn't want it too far away."

"Damien? I thought this was his wife's coat. Why would he hide her coat?" Even as he said it, Finn could hear his Granda's voice in his head say, 'Things are not always what they seem.'

"Look in holes in the ground or in old dead trees. Look between rocks and in caves. Look up into the trees and see if something is in the branches. Look any place you think it might be," Granda urged.

They scrambled over old logs and thick patches of bog land. They climbed in trees and looked under boulders. For more than two hours they looked in every place that they could think of, but there was no sign of the fur coat. Granda, looking glum and shaking his head, finally took Finn by the hand and headed back to the cottage.

"Granda, look at those giant strawberries!" said Finn who was feeling a bit peckish after all the hunting. Granda pulled at the netting that was keeping the birds away from the big red juicy treats in the cottage garden. He picked a strawberry for Finn and bit into one himself.

It was then that Finn noticed the old scarecrow in the corner of the patch, arms out- stretched and looking a little worse for wear. His head was an old football that had a badly painted face. His legs dangled and flopped in a pair of odd boots, one brown and one black. His body was an old oilskin raincoat that came to his knees and his hands looked like the gloves that Gran wore when she washed the dishes. Then, Finn noticed something that looked like hair jutting out through a rip in the side of the coat. Granda was bending down to pick another huge strawberry – this one almost as big as an apple – when Finn tapped him on the head and pointed. The old fella's eyes narrowed as he walked over to the scarecrow. He unbuttoned the oilskin and underneath was something that looked like a thick fur coat. "Very clever, Damian! Hide it in plain sight. Very clever!" Granda muttered. He quickly undressed the scarecrow and rolled the fur coat up, tucked it under his arm and quietly went back inside with Finn. The man and the boy sat on their makeshift beds in silence. Finn felt a bit giddy, but Granda looked angry so Finn popped his thumb in his mouth and tried not to fidget. He wanted to know what was so important about a scarecrow's old coat, but he sensed that this wasn't the time to ask that question.

Soon, there was the sound of pouring water, pots, pans and plates on the wooden table in the kitchen.

As they entered, Farraige was cooking a breakfast of toasted brown bread, eggs and bacon, while Damien drank steaming tea from a large brown mug. During breakfast, the usual "Good Morning," and "How did you sleep?" small talk was mixed with the slurping of tea, crunching of toast and the occasional yawn from Finn.

When the pleasantries were done, Granda asked, "So, Damien, do you ever get to spend time with Farraige's family? Where is it that they come from anyway?"

"Oh, we never see them. They live quite far away."

"Is that right? Galway? Limerick?"

Finn thought Damien looked irritated at Granda's question and noticed Farraige's hand begin to shake as she held the teapot to pour her husband another cup.

Granda continued. "I don't see any wedding pictures around the place. Sure, if any man was married to a woman as beautiful as your wife, you'd think they would be telling the world about it! You'd think that they would capture every moment so they could share it with their friends."

The big fisherman looked uncomfortable as the old man continued, "And sure, you'd be taking her out to every dance and restaurant in town to show everybody that you married the sweetest girl in the county. Surely you do that . . . surely you treat her like a princess so that everyone knows how much you love her?"

"It's none of your business what I do, old man. None of your business!"

At that, Granda reached around his chair and pulled out the fur coat. Damien's face turned red as Farraige drew a deep breath and sighed. Granda looked very, very angry.

"Really! You did this? This is slavery, don't ya know. Farraige is not your wife, is she? She is a prisoner in this house!"

Damien stood up from his seat and rolled up his sleeves. "I can do as I please, old man!" But, before he could even raise his hand, Granda had him pinned to the table and put one hand over the big man's big mouth.

"Is that so?" He turned his gaze to Farraige and spoke in a gentler voice.

"Take your coat and go home. The boy will make sure you get to the beach safely. Me and your man here have some business to attend to." She smiled and picked up the coat and looked at Finn as if to ask for permission to leave. Without thinking, he took her hand and the two of them headed towards the beach.

Granda whispered in the fisherman's ear, "So, it's the company of a house guest you want is it? When will you ever learn that you cannot take the Selkies as your slaves?[12] It's an offence in this world and it is an offence in the fairy world. It is an offence to everything good and pure . . . but if it's a companion you want, I can arrange for that alright!"

With that he let the big man go, but held his gaze until Damien slunked back and sat with his head down at the kitchen table.

---

12. Selkie, pronounced 'Sell-kee' – A magical water creature.

Finn and Farraige had hardly reached the beach when she asked him to look away for a moment. Finn did as he was asked and only turned back around when he heard her call his name. She was now dressed in the fur coat. It came all the way to the sand, covering her from neck to toe.

"Finn, there are no words that can thank you enough for what you and your grandfather have done for me. One day I will return that favour. A Selkie can never return to her home without her true skin. Thank you!"

With that, she pulled the hood of the fur coat over her head. Suddenly the coat began to change shape as if it was morphing and melting onto her body. In a moment, Farraige had taken the shape of a silver-grey seal and splashed into the sea where she vanished into the briny foam.

Finn stood speechless as he watched her disappear. He wondered if other boys had trips like this with their grandfathers.

He met Granda on the way back to the cottage and was about to tell him what he had just seen when the old man said, "I know. It is a sad truth that some men still think they can take what they want and use it for their own selfish greed. Learn a lesson here, Finny boy, no one is yours to own. Always act out of love." Finn nodded in agreement as the two continued on their way.

On the road, they met a very small man in a green suit with very shiny shoes who asked the way to Damien's cottage. Granda gave him directions and the little man sang as he went on his way. Finn laughed, "'He looked like a Leprechaun from one of your bedtime stories!"[13]

"Oh, that was no Leprechaun, Finny boy. That was a Clurichaun, one of the 'ne'r do well' cousins of the Leprechauns.[14] Greedy wee things, and as bad tempered as a bulldog chewing a wasp if they don't get their own way. I let it be known that Damien had a room spare. I think the big man will be more cautious about who he lets into his home when he's had that wee fella as a houseguest!" Granda winked and said, "Now, we have business to attend to!"

13. Leprechaun, pronounced 'Lep-re-con' – An Irish male fairy.
14. Clurichaun, pronounced 'Cloor-re-con' – A bad-tempered Irish male fairy.

Chapter Nine

# The Rath of King Colm

Whilst Finn and his Granda were helping the Selkie, there were even stranger things afoot for Evie; though, of course, at aged only two-and-a-bit, she woke every day to a new and exciting adventure. The little girl was therefore nothing but curious to find her slumber had this time delivered her into the peculiar, toylike land of Tara.

The fairy village was encircled by large oak trees, each with a tiny door at its roots. The whole place seemed to have a strange green glow all around it. Each miniature door lead to a hallway that became part of a series of tunnels leading to the underground Fairy Fort, which could be seen above ground in the shape of a grassy mound. Tiny torches lit the fort and each day, as the sun went down, the squeaky hinges on the little doors would open and the fairy people would begin their day. The tiny beings worked on all kinds of chores and some of them sang as they did so. One tree had a door that was larger than any other. It was in this ancient oak that the king lived. His doorway was just big enough to let a two-and-a-bit-year-old human girl inside. The king – His Royal Majesty King Colm – thought that he would be happy with his prize but, seeing her now, laying fast asleep on the full length of his royal banqueting table, he realised he had rather underestimated the size of human children. Evie snuffled and shuffled and even giggled in her sleep, which was fine in her princess bed in her human home, but here, the whole tree trunk palace vibrated with her sleepy purr, and King Colm feared he would be swallowed up in a spidery tangle of crazy red hair if she turned over quickly. Colm had commanded his army to make the room bigger for her but now, as she began to wake up, a look of terror filled his face. Evie stretched and knocked over every cup, plate and ornament in the room. Then she rolled over, opened one eye, then another, and looked at King Colm. He gulped and said, "Hello little human," but before he had finished, Evie picked him up by the neck (like she did with her dolls), stood up, pushed the door so hard it came off its hinges, stepped outside and laughed in delight at the tiny beings running around her.

One of the fairy soldiers shouted to his king, "Should we call the troops, your majesty?"

"No!" gasped King Colm. "You will most likely hurt me!" At that point, Evie spied some baskets of strawberries and abruptly dropped the king, landing him in a large pile of rather steamy fertilizer. The fairy community gathered around and watched Evie eat all of the fruit they had gathered for that week. She made strange noises like 'MMMM! HUMMFFFFP!

YUMMM! MMMMMGGGG!' and if any of them tried to get close, she would stop and stare at them until they backed off in fear!

It didn't take long for the giant red headed girl to finish off the strawberries, and with a long 'Buuuuurp!' she looked around to see what else might interest her. Very soon her eyes narrowed and her lips curled into a smile as she noticed the village supply of malt beer barrels stacked in a neat pile. "Poppy Pop's pop," she said with a grin, and the people scattered as she began trying to pluck a barrel from the bottom of the pile. King Colm, hands in front of his eyes, could only peek out between his fingers at the chaotic sight of the giant human baby covered in strawberry juice, giggling with delight at the soldiers as they ran and tripped over the rolling beer barrels. For Evie, it was one glorious game and she was very, very happy!

Chapter Ten

# Feeling a Little Horse

Finn was struggling to keep up. The previous night's adventure with a Selkie, a fur coat and a mean fisherman had allowed no sleep at all. He had witnessed a woman turn into a seal! He could almost smell the salt air as he remembered her splashing into the water and disappearing beneath the waves, back to her briny home. He wondered how many other boys his age had seen such a thing. All the excitement had kept the lad going, but he was feeling it now. The sun hadn't yet warmed the air and Finn shivered as the two travellers continued onwards. He was glad to find a pair of gloves that his mum had put in the pocket of his hooded jacket. Soon his fingers began to thaw out. The old man seemed to be as fresh as ever and kept a steady pace through the trees that skirted the coastline. After a good deal of time had passed, Granda suggested that they had a 'wee sit down' and maybe a bite to eat. Finn was happy with this idea. After another big apple, Granda said that he was going to look at the inside of his eyelids for a few minutes. Ten seconds later, he was gently snoring. Finn was glad of the rest and sat quietly looking out across the sea. In the distance, he noticed a large black figure splashing in the shallows. At first Finn thought of Farraige, the seal woman. Was it another of her kind? Finn glanced at his Granda but the old man slept on, his bushy eyebrows quivering in the breeze of his snore. The beast was coming closer. What if it was another of those horrible dog-like creatures, like the one that had attacked them in the woods? Was that only one night ago? So much seemed to have happened since then. No, this was no dog. It looked more like . . . like a horse. It splashed in the waves and rose out from the foam, its eyes flashing wide and proud as its strong flank powered towards the shore. Finn felt excitement run hot in his veins. "He sees us," he whispered. The grey dappled horse seemed to fix Finn in his gaze and, before he knew it, he could feel the warmth of its breath on his face. Black leather reigns hung around the animal's head as it stopped and looked straight into Finn's eyes.

Finn had ridden horses at summer camps and pony trekking schools. He knew that they could be dangerous, so he approached carefully. He wondered who owned the big grey stallion and what it was doing at the beach on its own. The reins hung temptingly in front of him and the horse's eyes seemed so inviting. Finn ached with tiredness. Would he be able to hop onto this horse? Finn surveyed it for a while and decided he would. He was the school high-jump runner up after all – beaten only by Fergus McBride, who had legs up to his neck and springs for feet. It would be a lot easier to ride than to walk. He reckoned there'd even be room for both him and Granda on the great stallion's back. Granda would be really pleased with him, Finn felt sure. They could ride the horse to the next town or village and leave it there for the owner. A brilliant idea!

He walked slowly towards the big animal, put one hand out and whispered, "Good boy. It's OK. No one is going to hurt you."

The horse snorted a little but stood perfectly still as Finn grabbed the reins. "You don't mind if I sit on your back and go for a wee ride, do you boy?" The animal seemed to nod in agreement as Finn grabbed its thick mane with one hand and leapt up to straddle the horse's back.

"NOOOOOOOO! Finn! No!" Granda jumped to his feet and lunged towards Finn and the horse, panic in his voice, but the horse suddenly jarred its head violently to one side, yanking the reins out of Finn's hand. Instinctively, Finn tightened his legs around the horse and buried his hands into its mane as it turned into a gallop.

Seawater splashed all around as the powerful beast charged along the shore. Finn looked back at his Granda, who actually seemed to be catching up with them. The horse changed course and began to head deeper into the sea. Soon the water was up to Finn's knees. The deeper water slowed the horse's gallop into a canter, then to a trot. Finn looked down at the waves. He could jump off now and get back to his Granda but, to his horror, he found that the horse's grey coat had a kind of sticky glue all over it. It clung greedily to the fabric of his trousers, keeping Finn firmly in place, and the boy realised that no matter how hard he tried, he couldn't wrench his hands free from the matted mane. The beast waded deeper into the water and soon the waves were licking around his shoulders. Deep beneath the horse's thick hair, Finn could make out three long slits on each side of its neck. They looked like the gills of a shark that Finn had seen in a picture when he was trying to figure out why he was called 'Finn'.

Suddenly, the horse whinnied, and his head snapped sharply round, his eyes blazing and startled. Finn was trying to blow water from his face when he saw Granda holding the leather bridal in both hands. "It's alright, Finn, I have the devil now!" Finn still couldn't see much for the spray of water, but he knew that the horse was trying to resist being pulled back to the shallows. It stiffened its legs and dug into the sandy seabed. The sand churned beneath the big hooves as the horse tried to pull himself and Finn back into the sea, but Granda kept his head pulled up and Finn saw the whites of the horse's eyes as it began to yield. Once again the old man's strong arms were more than a match for this adversary and soon they were back where the shallow waves lapped at the shore.

Granda tied the horse to a large piece of driftwood on the beach and shook his head as he looked at the big grey beast. "Stallion? More like hallion! You should pick on someone your own size!" The horse bowed his head with a look of equestrian shame as Granda continued,

"Finn, I need you to do exactly as I say. This steed you've been riding isn't any ordinary horse. This fine fellow is a Kelpie[15] and he usually stays in your home country of Scotland, but from time to time they pay us a wee visit here in the Emerald Isle. His coat, as you have discovered, is sticky and once you are stuck to it, you can't get off or escape."

Finn stared at Granda. He was right. No matter how much he tugged or squirmed, he couldn't get down from the horse.

"Don't ye worry my lad," Granda continued. "Today we have had some good Irish luck, so listen to every word I say!"

Finn couldn't help wondering how he was lucky at all! He couldn't get his hands or legs off the sticky hide no matter how hard he pulled. The old man walked to the side of the animal and, as he did, he whispered a warning in the Kelpie's pointy ear. "If you move a muscle, I will tie you to a tree in the forest far from the sea!" The horse seemed to understand and obeyed. "Finn, I need you to take your hands out of your gloves and leave them on the beast's back. Then, very carefully I want you to lean towards me and put your arms tightly around

15. Kelpie, pronounced 'Kel-pee' – A magical shape-shifting water creature.

my neck. Do not touch the Kelpie with your hands!" Finn slid his hands out of the gloves and did as he was bid. Granda reached around the boy's waist and with a mighty yank, he pulled Finn off the Kelpie, leaving most of his trousers and both of his boots stuck to the creatures back and sides. The old man held him in a tight Granda hug, the kind of hug that made you feel like nothing could hurt you. Granda set him down and looked at him sternly. "Oh Finn, don't go doing things like that. You need to think about your actions, even if you have good intentions. Not everything . . ."

". . . Is what it seems," finished Finn. "What about the Kelpie? What should we do about him?"

"When the tide comes in, he will be free to go back in the water," said Granda.

"But won't he do this again to someone else?"

Finn's Grandfather nodded a silent 'yes' then added, "Finn, the beasts simply do what they do, it's not their fault. It is us who must learn to respect them and take caution around them. You cannot blame a creature for being true to its nature."

They walked back to where they had stopped for a rest and Granda recovered his coat and backpack. He removed an old 'Zippo' lighter from one of the pockets in the bag, found some dry driftwood and lit a fire. After wrapping his dry coat around Finn, he said, "We will need to find you some new trousers and boots, boyo! I think I know the very place to get them."

## Chapter Eleven

# The Measure of A Man

The driftwood fire dried the two travellers out in no time at all and, as Granda packed his rucksack, he said, "Well boyo, you'll need to toss this on your back and climb up on my shoulders. You can't walk in these woods with no boots."

"Is there a shop close by where we can buy some new ones?" asked Finn.

The old man smiled. "Oh, I know a much better place, but we need to get going!"

Finn slung the canvas bag over his shoulder, squealing a little as Granda then flung him into the air, in pretty much the same way, to land him on his back. Finn wasn't exactly a big lad for his age, but it was amazing how his grandfather lifted him as though he was as light as a feather.

"Are you ready? We need to get moving." Finn nodded his head and, in a flash, they were off. Finn's eyes began to water in the wind and he clung tighter around Granda's neck. It was like being on the Kelpie again. Who would have thought that a grandfather could keep such speed, especially with a seven-year-old boy on his back! The sound of breaking branches, crackling dead leaves and the odd squelchy patch of bogland filled the forest as they sped through the trees. Occasionally a small branch slapped Finn on the head but Granda kept running. Finn began to hear other sounds joining the soundtrack to their journey. At first, it sounded like a 'clicking' noise, but as they got closer it was more like drumming. Soon the drumming was accompanied by the sound of voices singing in harmony. The voices were high-pitched but sang perfectly in tune. The drums seemed to have complicated, but brilliantly timed rhythms beating out an infectious groove. Finn's feet were tapping the air in time with the drums when Granda slowed down, as they came to an opening in the thick forest.

Granda unloaded Finn onto the greenest grass in the whole world and it was then that Finn realised they were somewhere very peculiar. He stared at the amazing, but slightly comical sight before his eyes. They were in a grass paddock surrounded by oak trees, each displaying a small wooden door with a large brass door handle and hinges. Stranger still, in the centre of the paddock, Finn spied twenty or more tiny men sitting at small wooden benches, with small hammers that they tapped in time onto pieces of leather. Each bench was scattered with thread, needles, nails, buckles and laces. A tiny set of tools sat neatly on each bench. There were small awls, petit pliers, itty-bitty blades, teeny thimbles and bars of weeny wax; at the end of each table was a small pile of tiny, perfectly made shoes. Two of the little men sat on small stools to one side of the shoemakers. One moved his bow across the strings of a fiddle in the fastest, most musical jig Finn had ever heard. The other skilfully kept time on a goatskin bodhrán. Finn recognised the woven knot design painted around the rim of the little hand drum. It was like some of the artwork in Granda and Gran's house.

All the little men were so happily engrossed in their work that they didn't notice their visitors. Granda and Finn stood quietly for a while watching their hammers swinging to the beat of their song,

*"We're the oldest*
*We're the finest*
*We're the best in all the land*
*We're the smartest*
*We're the brightest*
*And we have the finest band*
*For our music is our labour*
*And our work our happy song*
*For we do it and we love it*
*Sure now how could that be wrong?"*

"Ahem! Where can some weary travellers find a bite to eat, a drink and maybe some new clothes?" The hammering stopped in unison as all eyes turned to peer at the two strangers. One of the little men jumped onto his workbench. He was dressed in a green suit with trousers that came to his knees. Finn noted the red and white striped socks seamlessly joining the bottom of his trousers. On his feet were the shiniest black leather shoes Finn had ever seen. Each shoe had a big silver buckle that matched the belt buckle holding his trousers in place. The little man took off his large green cloth hat and threw it on the bench as he rolled up his sleeves, spat on the ground and shouted to Granda, "So, you think yer a big man do ye? If ye can beat me in an arm wrestle, maybe we can discuss your request! Oh, an' I see ye still have that watch . . . I'd like that back!" The field grew quiet as Granda walked towards the leprechaun and sat crossed legged on the grass by the bench.

"Yer on, wee man!" he said, with a determined grin.

The leprechaun clenched a small clay pipe between his teeth and half shut one eye. "You big lads are all the same, and don't be thinkin' that ye can steal our gold again! I'll teach you a lesson!"

Granda's big fist closed around the tiny man's hand and someone from another bench yelled something that sounded like, "Tree . . . Two . . . Wun . . . GO!" The miniature musicians started playing a furious reel as Granda and the little man tensed their muscles to begin their tabletop battle. Finn laughed as he watched the spectacle, but soon stopped sniggering as the other tiny men gave him hard stares. His grandfather looked so huge beside the leprechaun, and Finn knew that the old man was strong as ten horses. Surely, the wee man had no chance of winning. Finn thought about what kind of boots he might like when his Granda won the contest, but then he noticed big beads of sweat on the old fella's forehead.

"Ya wee hallion ye! Have you been working out?"

The wee man smiled and grunted a little as he pushed Granda's arm closer to the table.

"I will leather ya at this game, big lad!" Granda snorted and pushed hard forcing the leprechaun's arm back in the other direction. For more than ten minutes, the grunting and moaning continued as each man's arm was pushed left and right. Insults such as, *"Hallion!", "Ya wee Devil!", "Ya big dumpling*!" filled the air, until eventually the two competitors nodded and let go of each other's strong hands. They sat for a moment staring, and then suddenly began roaring with laughter.

"Och, I've missed you, big fella! How long has it been?"

"Too long, wee man," replied Granda as he beckoned Finn over to the table. "Finn, meet Big Fergus Connor, the chief of this fine group of leprechauns. Fergus, meet Finn, my grandson!"

Fergus held out his tiny hand and shook Finn's hand vigorously.

"Finn, eh? Any signs that you have some of the old fella's special quirks, young'un?"

"Not really," said Finn, rubbing his aching hand. "I'm just an ordinary boy."

Granda scoffed. "An ordinary boy who had a visit from the banshee a few days ago!"

"Is that a fact now?" said the leprechaun, with his eyebrows disappearing up into his freshly placed hat. "Well, we shall see what the future has for you young Finn." He beckoned Finn to bend down a little so he could whisper closer to his ear. "I can tell the future, y'know."

"Really?"

"Yes, really. For instance, I know that some new breeches and boots are in your future!" The entire group of tiny men erupted with laughter and soon hammers were clicking and songs were ringing out across the paddock.

Some of the little men (who were all dressed pretty much in the same kind of clothing) brought tiny plates of food for their guests. There were mushrooms and mixed nuts accompanied by bowls of potatoes and hot dandelion tea. The plates were small but the food was fresh and delicious. Finn had twelve platefuls and Granda a few more. Fergus was charming and funny, although he did get a little cross when Finn suggested that his Granda had allowed Fergus to last so long in the arm wrestle.

His eyebrows shifted to the 'ten minutes to two' position on his forehead and he grumbled, "You boyos always think that bigger is stronger, but not everything is what it seems y'know!" Finn apologised and explained that he was learning new things every day. Fergus accepted the apology and continued, "You know the boyo that you are named after was one of Ireland's great heroes. Now *he was* a big lad, as big as your Granda, and he did some mighty things!" Finn looked at his Granda who stood five foot seven in his stocking feet.

"Granda's not big!" laughed Finn, but the little man butted in, "Well that depends what you measure him against. Finn McCool was five foot eight inches high. A giant of a man!"

Finn was confused. "Five foot eight isn't tall!"

"Well, we were there, and we wrote the stories. A man five foot eight is a giant of a man if you are a leprechaun. Great people are not always tall people. Never measure a person's greatness by their size from their feet to their head. Measure how big they are by the size of their acts of love, courage, fairness and bravery. Measure them by the size of their good heart boyo!"

Just then, a little man called Nub appeared with a pair of leather breeches, a pair of lovely leather gloves and a shining pair of leather boots. The trousers fitted Finn perfectly and the boots felt as though they had been made for him.

"We made these for you," said Nub.

"How did you know my size?"

Nub answered, "It's what we do, and we do it well!" Then he walked back to his bench and began hammering and singing.

Granda pulled on his jacket and said, "Thank you for the food and clothes, Fergus, but we must make haste. The changelings have taken my granddaughter to Tara. What is the fastest way from here?

"Well now," answered Fergus, "if I was you, I wouldn't want to go to Tara from here!" Granda rolled his eyes. "It's a good day's walk for sure," the leprechaun continued, "and you need to watch the woods at night. Maybe even see if Gaoth could direct you."[16]

"Gaoth? I am sure she is busy with other things."

"Well now, in my experience she is never too busy to point us in the right direction!" Granda nodded his head and shook Fergus by the hand. Fergus hugged Finn and whispered, "I shall look forward to seeing what else the future has for you, Finn."

As they headed into the forest, a soft breeze blew Finn's hair into his eyes. A large shadow darkened their path for a moment, then vanished into the trees to the north and seemed to cause the leaves on the trees to shake and rustle. Fergus shouted out, "Well now, doesn't that look like Gaoth is giving you a hint that you are on the right path?"

"It does that," said Granda. "It does that."

---

16. Gaoth, pronounced 'Ga-wee' – Wind.

Chapter Twelve

# The Work, The Word and The Wind

The leprechaun breakfast had given Finn and Granda some energy for the journey and even though Finn was feeling a little tired, he strode out with good vigour in his new boots and trousers. By noon, the sun had warmed the forest. The birds competed for the lead part in the chorus and every fern and wildflower looked like it was stretching out in joy of life.

"Who is Gaoth?" asked Finn as they walked further through the woodland.

Granda dropped his backpack from his shoulder and pulled out his old book. "Well lad, it's sometimes hard to make sense of the world around us. There are mysteries for sure. We have a brain in our head to help us solve some, but the truth is, we just don't

know everything. The universe is amazing, full of incredible sights, sounds, smells, tastes and more. The Old Ways tell us that there are three great powers that help us make sense of it: The Work, The Word and The Wind. They never act alone, always together. The Work made everything that exists. You can get glimpses of The Work in everything natural that is around, and if you really pay attention, you can even find Him working inside you!" Finn furrowed his brow as he walked along, trying to make sense of his Granda's words. He was used to the old man talking in riddles.

"The Word is the one who points us to The Work," Granda continued. "The Word explains, instructs, defines, corrects and encourages us. He is poetry and song, literature and music. Every rhythm and sound, birdsong and crash of a wave whispers The Word to us. The Word never ends and never stops informing us and speaking to us. There is nowhere that you can go where you can escape Him. The Word is everywhere."

Finn nodded, though he was still struggling to understand. Why did Granda talk about a Word as *He*?

"Finally, there is The Wind. You can't often see her but you feel her," Granda said, looking wistfully into the air. "Sometimes she gently calms us but, at other times, she is a raging storm that shakes us. The Wind is always around us, always near us and always ready to blow us in the right direction. The

Wind's name is Gaoth and if she reveals herself, she does so as a gigantic Wild Goose. She is wild and free. The Wild Goose crosses any border she pleases without permission and she brings both comfort and conviction on all people. Her goal is to make us all the best that we can be. She never acts without the help of The Work and The Word, but you must never take her for granted. She has strength more than you can ever imagine. Geese can win a fight with a fox y'know, so don't imagine that Goath is always polite and gentle. She has been known to get a little 'forceful' when things are not going in the right direction!" Finn screwed up his face until he had little wrinkles on his nose – his 'confused' face.

"Should I be frightened of her?" Finn asked.

"No, Finn, but you should show her respect!" They stopped as Granda lifted his face to the sky, closed his eyes and began to recite a poem with a tone to his voice that was so beautiful that even the birds stopped singing just so they could listen.

*"Open up your eyes child*
*Wake up from your sleep*
*And see the sun arise once more*
*And see the ocean deep*
*And see the wooded forest*
*Who made its leafy tree?*
*The Work, The Word, the Wind*
*The blessed Holy Three.*

*And gaze upon the mountains*
*And gaze upon the stars*
*And gaze upon the old Ireland*
*From Bray to Mullingar,*
*Clonmacnoise or Galway*
*They bid us all to see,*
*The Work, The Word, the Wind*
*The blessed Holy Three."*

Finn felt goosebumps on his skin and looked up to the blue sky, thinking that he might catch a glimpse of a giant wild goose bursting through the clouds. But the sky was still and the only sound in the forest was Granda's steady voice.

*"All that we can see and touch*
*All that we can hear*
*All that we can smell and taste*
*Unite to draw us near*
*Compelling us to listen*
*To taste and smell and see,*
*The Work, The Word, the Wind*
*The blessed Holy Three.*

*So in my joys and trials*
*And in my fear or pain*
*If I see through eyes of faith*
*I'll surely see again,*
*That I live in amongst them*
*And they live in me*

*The Work, The Word, the Wind*
*The blessed Holy Three."*

The entire forest seemed to wait in stillness as Granda finished the poem. He kept his eyes closed for a few moments and Finn thought that he saw a small tear run down the old man's cheek. When Granda opened his eyes, Finn noticed the birds were taking up to their chirpy tunes and the woodland, once again, was filled with the rustle of small creatures hurrying back to their woodland business.

Granda handed the book to Finn. "This is for you, son. Read it and pay heed to it."

"But Granda, this is your book. Your favourite book! I can't take it," Finn protested.

The old man smiled. "You take it, boyo. I have been reading it all my life and know it off by heart. It's not the paper that's important but The Word, the story, the meaning and the lessons. They are deep in my heart and mind. Anyway, I can get another book, but you should have this one."

Finn took the old book in both hands. It had a reddish-brown leather cover with a silver Celtic 'Trinity' Knot on the front. He ran his fingers around the lines of the knot, noticing how they wove in a seemingly endless pattern. He could smell the leather and a faint hint of tobacco from the times Granda would smoke his pipe as he read (Gran told him to stop because it was bad for his health and bad for her nose!). Underneath the knot it said 'THE

BOOK' in silver writing, although some of the letters looked cracked and broken. Finn flicked through the pages as they walked and Granda occasionally grabbed him by the collar to stop him falling down a hole or walking into a tree. The pages looked as if they had been turned many times. Thumbprints and stains scarred many of them, yet somehow added to its beauty and sense of wonder. Finn knew it was an important book to his Granda and asked, "Is this book worth a lot of money?"

"No, Finn, it's just ordinary paper, ink and leather, but if you are asking if it is valuable then the answer is yes, it's more valuable than you can guess right now. Not everything of worth is measured by money, there are some things that money cannot buy and the quicker you learn that, the wiser a boy you will be!"

Finn understood what the old man meant. His mother had often told him that love, family, kindness and fairness were all worth more than money.

Finn closed the book carefully. He suddenly felt that he had been given some priceless treasure. "I promise I'll always keep it safe," he said very seriously to Granda.

The old man smiled. "I know you will my boy. Now, how about we put it back in the bag for safekeeping and make haste to Tara. Who knows what sort of chaos your sister is causing among them fairy folk!"

## Chapter Thirteen

# It's a Dog's Life

The pair walked on until Finn's head started to droop and his legs ached with trying to keep up with Granda's big strides. Eventually, when he thought he couldn't walk a step further, they stopped and sat down on the grass. The sound of running water came from somewhere through the trees. When curiosity got the better of weariness, Finn picked himself up and headed towards the sound.

"Finn, wash your face in the cold water. It will wake you up for sure!" called Granda.

Finn smiled and headed through the trees. It only took a few minutes to find the bubbling stream and a small waterfall. Finn knelt by the bank and splashed the water on his cheeks and eyes. It was freezing cold but did a fine job of waking him up. He lifted his head back to let the sun dry his wet face. It felt good.

A sudden crack, and then a noise something like heavy breathing, made Finn spin around. Blinking water from his eyes, he swallowed hard, feeling the hair on the back of his neck prickle. There, in the trees, he picked out the form of something large and beastlike. Two big yellow eyes stared out from a dog-like face that was covered in matted brown hair. Finn gulped. The yellow discs stared directly at him. Finn, rooted to the spot, stared too. It must only have been a split second, but in that time, Finn studied the fangs that jutted out from the creature's gnarly mouth. The beast stood upright, like a man, but its features were largely that of a dog, or was it a bear? Finn wouldn't consider for too long. Whatever it was, it looked like it meant business, and – from the way it started to breathe heavier and move towards him, all lumbering and menacing – Finn doubted that its business could be anything good.

Suddenly the beast dropped down low and growled at the boy. Finn made a quick assessment, noting the beast's muscular hind legs and wolf-like upper torso. To run at this stage would be pointless. Fighting to stay calm, he moved to his left in an attempt to make a wide circle around his opponent. But when he moved, the beast mirrored him, blocking his way. Finn moved to the right and the same thing happened but this time the beast came towards him at the same time. There was nothing for it . . .

'RUN!' Finn's brain yelled to his legs and his skinny limbs pounded harder than ever before as Finn hurtled towards a gap in the trees.

The hound-thing gave chase, snapping at his ankles. Finn was one of the fastest runners in his class at school, but no matter how fast he ran now, the beast stayed close. Tree branches swished and slapped his face and Finn's heart thumped loudly in his surely-soon-to-explode chest. He could feel the beast's breath and knew the sharp fangs were inches from his legs. Finn was a clever boy and he'd watched a lot of chase scenes in movies. By instinct, he suddenly stopped quickly and jumped behind a large oak tree, hoping that the beast would just keep going on by.

It didn't. Now Finn was caught, his back up against the tree trunk, his fingers digging into the bark as the beast came to a stop in front of him, its sharp claws cutting furrows into the dirt.

"Fight or flight," thought Finn and, again by instinct more than reason, he took off to his right, speeding towards a rocky outcrop, his eyes almost blinded by the sweat streaming off his forehead and the 'thump, thump, thump' of his heart keeping time with his pounding legs. The dirt and gravel gave no traction (even to his amazing leprechaun boots) and Finn soon found himself, with a thud, face down in tiny stones and clay. The snarling noise behind him was closing in and Finn looked around for something that might help. He remembered his Granda's words during the fight with the black dog: "You will find that most everything you need is closer than you think!" There was grass within reach. He tore it from the earth and wrapped it around his fist. As he spun his body around, the beast was upon him and with a loud scream Finn swung his fist and hit the thing square on the jaw. It stopped and, for a moment, the world went silent. The beast looked down at Finn as if nothing more than a flea had landed on its face. "I'm a goner now," Finned muttered to himself as one long slimy slobber slipped from the beast's mouth and slowly dangled down towards his face. Just then, a shrill whistle attracted the beast's attention. It turned its hairy head (the jerking motion made the slobber break off and land right on Finn's nose) towards the place where Granda was casually tossing his tennis ball into the air and catching it over and over. Finn, incredulous, began wiping slime off his face, not daring to take his eyes off the beast. Then, Granda threw the ball, not at the beast, but far in the other direction. The great hound-thing watched the ball fly through the air, then, like a family pet dog, bolted after it. Moments later, it returned to Granda with the ball in its slobbery mouth. The old man scratched its head, grabbed the spit-covered ball and threw it again. The beast ran off and returned wagging its tail and panting.

Finn picked himself up and dashed gravel and grit from his clothes. "What is that thing, Granda?"

"This is a Conriocht. You might have heard of its kind, sometimes they are called Werewolves."[17]

Finn gulped. "W . . . w . . . Werewolves? Aren't they dangerous? Don't they eat children?"

Granda smiled as he scratched the strange dog's belly, for it was now lying on its back with its legs in the air! "You've been watching too much TV lad," scoffed Granda. "The Conriocht can be trouble for sure, but not to children. They are sworn to protect all children from danger when they can. This old girl was just trying to drive you out of the woods because she knows it can be a dangerous place for a young boy!"

"Girl? . . . Protect me?!" stammered Finn incredulously. "But she was biting at my ankles!"

"Aye, the way a sheep dog snaps at the flock to push them in the right direction. She won't hurt you Finn and furthermore, she won't let anyone else hurt you if she can help it! C'mere and scratch her head." Finn nervously walked towards the beast. He let her sniff his fist before stroking her hairy neck. Soon she was rolling in the dirt and making a funny squeaking sound as Granda and Finn scratched and played with her like she was a puppy.

"Some things that seem frightening aren't so bad at all, are they, boyo?" Finn had to agree. Granda took the beast's head in both hands and looked deep into the yellow eyes. "Thank you for

17. Conriocht, pronounced 'Con-richt' – A werewolf.

protecting my grandson, Conriocht. You are good and kind!" The hair on the beast's face receded and its fangs grew smaller as it looked at the old man. To Finn's amazement, it soon looked more like the face of a beautiful, but sad, young woman. She tilted her head in the way a dog does when it seems confused and whispered, "Why is the boy in the forest? Where are you going?"

"Changelings have taken his sister to Tara, we need to get her back," said Granda, picking bits of dirt out from under his fingernails.

"A quest to save a child! There is no nobler a quest. Let me travel with you, let me be your companion," spoke the low husky voice of the she-wolf.

Finn grabbed his grandfather's jacket sleeve and exclaimed, "But Granda, she is a Werewolf . . . she is not like us!"

Granda smiled down at him. "Yes, she looks and behaves differently than we do Finn, that much is true, but if you look into her eyes you can see that her heart and intentions are as good as ours. Do not judge someone by how they look, but rather check the good that their heart makes them do. This is a better measure."

Finn looked at the she-wolf's face. It was sad, but kind. Their eyes locked for a moment and it was as if Finn had looked into the face of a brave and trusted old friend. The old man smiled at his grandson. "It's your decision, boy."

Finn spoke to the she-beast. "What is your name?"

"When I was a woman I went by the name of Aileen." Her gaze fell, as though she were somehow ashamed.

Finn knelt and looked her in the eye, whispering, "Aileen, walk with us. I will feel much safer with you at our side."

Aileen smiled, her face softening and her eyes glinting. Slowly it changed once again into the face of a beast, as a very human tear ran down her cheek. Finn too sniffled a dribble from his nose and thought he caught Granda discretely wiping his eyes as the three set off toward Tara.

Chapter Fourteen

# Milk and Honey

Evie had eaten all the strawberries and other fruit that she could find. The little people stayed at a distance, nervously watching her. The soldiers had their swords drawn, waiting for command. By now, King Colm had managed to climb out of the pile of dung that Evie had unknowingly dropped him in and got most of the manure off his green velvet coat. He adjusted his little golden crown and, taking a deep breath to try to restore his dignity, he addressed Evie.

"Now then, young lady, we have some rules around here and it's time you knew what they . . ."

Evie giggled at the little man and picked him up by the neck once again. Her eyes were drawn to his golden crown. Evie liked crowns. They looked like the ones in the princess cartoons she watched. She chuckled and cooed as she grabbed the king's crown and plopped on top of her curly red mop. Evie didn't realise that, in her excitement about the crown, that she was squeezing the king's neck a little harder. Now his eyes were bugged out and he was frantically waving his legs and arms around like a distressed beetle. The king's army ran towards the giant, swords raised and chanting a war cry. The king tried to tell them to stand down, but Evie was crushing his neck so tightly that all he managed was, "Staa doon ugh mmmm!" The soldiers got closer as Evie picked up a huge branch with her other hand. With one swipe, she sent all the little warriors flying. Some hit trees and little wooden doors, others rolled and came to a halt on the grass, and one or two disappeared into the forest. Evie screamed and laughed as she swiped and brushed the tiny people with her branch. Just when King Colm was turning blue, Evie noticed barrels full of creamy milk and tiny jars of golden, syrupy honey. She dropped the king into another dung heap that smelled worse than the first one. She picked up the barrels one at a time and slurped the milk. No one dared stop her gulping down all their supply of milk, although she did share some with the king in the form of large drops that landed on his head. Soon she was licking the last of the honey from the final jar. When she had finished, she looked all around her very slowly and smiled. The king became very afraid and wondered, "What is she thinking now?"

Chapter Fifteen

# The Dark Fool

Back in the forest, the three travellers had not gone far when they met two men coming from the opposite direction. One was dressed in brightly coloured clothes. His jacket was red on one side and white on the other. His trousers were the same, but the colours were on opposite sides. He wore a floppy red cap, perched on top of thick, brown, wavy hair. His boots were different colours and styles; one looked like a brown brogue while the other a black shoe with a silver buckle. The man had long thin fingers with a ring on each one, even his thumbs! He carried a tin whistle in his right hand. His companion had a silly grin on his face and looked as though he might have had too much whiskey. He was dressed entirely in a brown suit covered in dark stains, and a pair of dirty brown boots. His shirt was a grey shade of white and a dirty green tie hung loosely around his neck.

"Tidings of joy and blessings of the day upon you my three friends!" sung the ring-fingered man in an oddly high-pitched voice. Finn thought that his scarlet lips looked even redder due to the paleness of his face. Even though he smiled, there was something uncomfortable in the air and Finn's instinct told him this stranger was not to be trusted. There was just something sinister about him, but Finn tried to remember his Granda's advice about not judging someone by the way they first appear.

"How are ya?" replied Granda.

"Hello," said Finn, politely.

Aileen rumbled a low growl, making the white-faced man step back a little.

"Well now, where would you fine fellows and, errrr, the 'doggie', be heading this fine day?"

Granda looked the man up and down, then stared at his companion for a moment before answering, "Och, just some family business."

"How about a quick cup of tea and maybe a story or two? My name is Darcy and I am a storyteller."

Granda's eyes narrowed and he replied, "We are in something of a hurry, we don't have time for stories today."

"No time for a story? There is always time for a story, sure, the story is all that we have!" Darcy reached his hand out to stop Granda as he began to walk on by, but the old man stepped back before the bony fingers could touch him.

"Well, on second thoughts, perhaps a mug of tea and a short story would help us on our way," said Granda quietly, his eyes fixed on the stranger. Darcy smiled, his red lips stretching from ear to ear.

"I will gather some wood to light a fire. A story is always best by a good fire!"

Granda smiled and nodded as the strange man and his companion gathered twigs and branches. He turned to Finn and Aileen and whispered, "Now, hear me you two. This one's stories will be charming and enthralling but whatever you do, do not touch his skin or allow his skin to touch yours! Do you hear me?" Finn nodded and Aileen wagged her tail. Granda pulled his old leather gloves on and told Finn to do the same.

Soon a fire was crackling and roaring as water bubbled steaming hot in an old Billie Can. Darcy placed the tin whistle between his thin red lips and began to play. A cheerful tune filled the air and Darcy's companion (whom he had not yet introduced) began to dance very badly.

The storyteller began his tale in rhyme.

*"It was so very long ago*
*that men and women dreamed*
*that life would be much easier*
*than their life now seemed.*
*If only they could have no cares*
*If they could have no woe*
*Surely they'd give anything*
*This knowledge for to know."*

Finn thought it a rather odd song and he realised he was digging his fingers nervously into the fur around Aileen's neck. He was glad for her presence.

*"A simple life was out of reach*
*For every man did know,*
*You needed money, land and wealth*
*To make your problems go,*
*And sure that meant more work and toil*
*More pain and misery*
*A simple life was harder*
*Than the life they had, you see?"*

Finn glanced over at Granda, who was rubbing his left thumb into the palm of his right hand, the way he always did when he was pondering something.

*"But what if one could come along*
*Who knew another way*
*A way that took no toil or work*
*That kept their fears at bay*
*A way that changed your thinking*
*A way that changed your mind.*
*A way to see things differently*
*Free from daily grind."*

Finn sensed Granda beginning to grow tense as the song went on.

*"The man who tells the stories*
*The man who quotes the rhyme*
*As old as any memory*
*Drawn from the dawn of time*
*His stories will enchant you*

*His poems will enthral*
*But he is never happy 'till*
*He touches one and all!"*

Darcy's companion let out a long chilling moan and began to shake. He tried to say something, but no words formed in his open mouth. Darcy set his whistle down and suddenly reached to grab Finn, but Aileen was faster. She clamped her strong fangs around the storyteller's jacket sleeve and held fast. Darcy tried to get hold of the hound's neck but Granda grasped his other arm with his gloved hands. Aileen and Granda held Darcy's arms outstretched as he struggled and twisted. His companion began to dance and laugh as the storyteller grew red with rage.

"Let go of me, old man, or there will trouble!"

"Oh, there will be trouble alright, Amadán![18] One word from me and the Conriocht will have your arm for dinner. You know she is sworn to protect children and if you don't fear her, then give some thought to what a grandfather will do to protect his own!" Aileen growled and slobbered as if she would relish dining on the storyteller's skinny arm.

Darcy screamed, "If you so much as brush your skin on mine, you will be 'touched'. Your mind will have no more worries until the day you die! Isn't that what you want?"

18. Amadán, pronounced 'Om-a-daun' – Dark fool.

Granda tightened his grip, pinning the storyteller by the shoulders and looking him in the eye. "For my grandson I would take any pain, even your twisted 'gift' of 'peace of mind'. You are no more than a robber of dreams and hope, your gift is a curse, but today you have met your match. Life must have its trials and battles, its joys and its happiness. These are the things that *make* a life. What you offer is a dullness that takes everything away from us . . .'

"Go on, Granda!" whispered Finn, excitedly. He loved it when the old man preached like this.

"Passion, love, rage, intelligence, real people, true grit, trials and triumphs . . . no, I don't want your 'peace'. I choose life!" By now, Granda's face was right up against Darcy's face and Finn could see the stranger beginning to cower in the wake of the old man's spittle-spewing sermon. Aileen pulled on his sleeve harder and growled louder still.

With one last attempt at a threat, Darcy coughed out the words, "You can't kill me! The story goes on forever!"

"True," said Granda, "but I can tell the story too. In this story you could be bound in a dark hole in the forest for the next five hundred years . . . how does that sound?"

"Arggghhh! Alright, alright! Let me go and I will be on my way with no harm to you," screamed Darcy, now almost breathless with rage-filled defeat.

"That is not enough for me!" snarled Granda. "Your companion, release him and set him free!"

Darcy spat back, "I have already touched him, he has no cares! Why would I take that away from him?'

Aileen's nose wrinkled up as if she was about to attack. The old man said firmly, "Give him back his choice and his own free will to make his own mistakes. A man should choose his own way!"

The storyteller glanced at the wolf then at the old man's steely eyes. "Very well . . . but he won't be happy!"

"Well that will be his own doing then, not yours."

Darcy spoke a simple rhyme, his voice weak in defeat.

*"Back to all your troubles friend*
*Back to all your stress*
*Back to all the things that made*
*Your worthless life a mess.*
*Back to all your arguments*
*Back to all your strife*
*Back to weary hardship*
*That you once called your life!"*

Granda shook his head as he listened to Darcy's sad definition of life. "Oh storyteller, there is so much more," he whispered to himself.

The man in the dirty brown suit began to cry. Finn held his breath and tried to stop his own eyes from doing that prickly thing they did when watching a sad movie. Then, he noticed the strange little man beginning to shake. He shoulders heaved and he made a strangled gasping sound, but very soon Finn realised that these were not sobs of distress. No! The man was now laughing! And, just as his tears were infectious, his laughter was even more so. Finn, though still confused, found he was smiling, then laughing too as he watched the man's face light up with laughter, his dirty, pale skin now flushed with joyful colour. The once sad eyes now twinkled and danced and he touched Granda and Finn gratefully on the shoulder and scratched Aileen's head before he ran off shouting,

"Thank you, sir! Thank you, wolf! Thank you, boy! I will make my life the best it can be, for myself and for others . . . the very best it can be! Thank you!"

They watched him disappear into the forest before turning their attention back to Darcy.

"I will be letting you go now, but the wolf will stay with you until we are out of your reach," the old man said sternly. "You should remember, she will die for the sake of the boy and while she may not be able to end your story, she can make sure it has a distressing chapter for you!" Darcy nodded in defeat as the old man loosened his grip on him. Then Granda picked up his walking stick and backpack and took Finn by the hand.

"There is another story that instructs us in the way of true peace, Darcy," said Granda, more gently now. "It is the one that I choose freely and the one that I pass on to my children and grandchildren and anyone else who will listen!"

Darcy stood silent as they backed away. Aileen's grip remained firm until the two vanished into the woods. Only then did she let go of the storyteller and run after her companions.

Chapter Sixteen

# Nobody Puts Baby in the Corner

King Colm was brushing yet more dung off his breeches when his general (who was called Stump and had a very squashed up face) approached him with a look of panic in his eyes.

"Yer majesty, we need to do somethin' about the human child. Soon we will have no food left and she is wreckin' everything she touches!"

"Did you imagine that I hadn't noticed?" snapped the frustrated monarch. "What would you suggest, General Stump?" The general's face contorted into an even more squashed visage and he rubbed his pointy red beard and puffed a long clay pipe for a moment.

"Now, maybe if we can get her into a corner we could somehow secure her with ropes for a while. Just until she calms down a bit?"

The King nodded and made, 'Emmm Hmmm' sounds for a moment. "Very well, General. Do what you must to save our home and our food supply!"

The general saluted and called on his men to form a line in front of the giant baby girl. The little soldiers looked terrified, since many of them were still sore from Evie's branch attack. With a wave of his arm, General Stump shouted, "Advance!" and his miniature military men raised their swords and yelled in unison, "HO! HAAA!" Evie looked down at them as they moved towards her and took two steps backwards.

"It's working," said General Stump. "Now we just need to corner her."

"Err . . . how can we trap her in a corner when our home is a Rath?" asked King Colm, slapping his palm to his forehead in frustration. "It's a circle, isn't it? A Ringed Fort! No corners!"

The General was about to give a ridiculous answer when he saw Evie smile and begin to laugh. She was enjoying this game. The little giant girl took one step forward, then jumped right over the army. As she landed behind them, she spun around and began to kick dirt and pebbles at the little men. Tiny rocks bounced off their heads, dirt and soil blinded them for a moment and then, quite mischievously, Evie kicked the large, steaming pile of manure (the same one that the king has been dropped in earlier) all over the troops. The soldiers gagged and balked as bits of manure got stuck in their teeth and clung to their uniforms. Evie roared with laughter.

"How is she so strong and fast?" The king demanded of his general.

"I don't know, Sire. Normally we can outsmart humans. There is something odd about this one!" The general said, wiping poo off his face and watching his soldiers rubbing their eyes and making sounds like, "Irk! . . . Gaaach! . . . Bleech!" and "I want my mummy!"

Evie laughed so hard that she fell on her back and kicked her legs in the air. Then she turned her head and looked at the king and General Stump. They both made a loud 'gulping' noise in unison.

Chapter Seventeen

# Cliff and The Shadows

Granda, Finn and Aileen had made good time since leaving the creepy storyteller behind. The old fella looked at the boy and the she-wolf and said, "Not far now, but the closer we get to Colm's Kingdom in Tara, the more trouble you can expect. I do wonder why that wee hallion has taken Evie. I suspect there is more to it than getting a queen!"

The trio travelled further until they came to higher ground, where a cooler breeze tickled their faces with salty air. The path narrowed and skirted a cliff edge with a death-defying drop into a raging ocean below. Seabirds cawed and cried as they circled above. Finn thought how great it would be to be able to fly so high and view the world below. Aileen kept herself just behind the boy at his right heel. Her wolf mind was thinking, "This lad will end up in the sea in a minute," as she watched Finn walking with his face looking upwards and giving no thought to where his feet fell. Finn could hardly keep his eyes off the mesmerising white birds, especially when he noticed one large, black bird circling a little higher than the rest.

"What kind of sea bird is that, Granda?" he asked.

The old man shielded his eyes from the sun with his left hand and looked upwards. As he did so, the large black bird swooped down and almost hit Finn with its sharp beak. It flew high again, then closed its powerful wings and dropped once more. Startled, Finn realised the bird was flying right at him, its pointy black beak like an arrowhead. He ducked and covered his face with his arms. In a flash, Granda swung his Blackthorn Shillelagh and connected with the bird's body. It squawked and tumbled to the ground, but shook its head and turned a black beady eye on Finn once again. The bird flapped its powerful wings but before it could get more than a few inches off the ground, Aileen had it in her jaws. She held tight then shook her head violently from side to side and threw the bird over the edge of the cliff.

Finn gasped with relief as he watched the bird plummet into the sea.

"Why would a bird attack me?" he asked, breathless with shock.

Aileen's face changed partially into the face of a woman so she could speak. She looked at Granda and said one word. "Sluagh!"[19]

"If you are right, Aileen, then this is just the beginning," the old man said as he began scanning the

19. Sluagh, pronounced 'Slew-ha' – Horde/crowd.

sky. "Sluagh always come in hordes. That hallion was just a scout!" Aileen nodded in agreement and returned to her wolf form.

Finn was confused. "What is a Sluagh? Wasn't it just a big raven?" Finn registered a look on the old man's face that concerned him.

He replied, "The Sluagh can look like ravens, for sure, but they are much more sinister. The Sluagh are a horde of the vilest things in the fairy world. They attack in flocks and they are merciless. If I am right and they come again, there may be too many of them. We won't be able to drive them off . . . not just three of us."

"But Granda, you must know a way to beat them? There must be a way!"

The old man shook his head and said, "They are drawn to us when we feel lost or lonely; when our hearts know fear and hopelessness. It is these things we must guard against if we are to defeat them. If they come as a horde, the only way to be saved is to put someone else in their path. To survive, you must sacrifice another."

Finn did not like this story and whimpered, "But how can we not be afraid and hopeless when you say that we cannot beat them, or that someone else must suffer?"

Granda looked at his grandson and smiled. "I said that we couldn't drive them off, not just the three of us!" As he spoke, a dark shadow splashed across them for a moment. Finn ducked down, fearing that it was another raven, but then he saw his Grandfather smile and Aileen bow her head.

"Don't be afraid of every shadow, boyo. Even shadows are given form by light. Sometimes they are just letting us know that we are not alone. Now, let's make haste before it gets dark. We need to get Evie home!"

## Chapter Eighteen

# Play Time

Evie had just got back on her feet and started to walk towards King Colm and General Stump.

"Should I call the men to arms?" asked the general. King Colm looked around at his battered and bruised army and wondered what Evie might do if she got angry instead of playful.

"Perhaps not just now. Let's see what she wants to do first." The enormous baby girl walked towards the little men, giggled then walked straight past (much to their relief). She had noticed some musical instruments sitting on a large table near one of the little doors on a big oak tree. Tiny fiddles and bodhráns, some small marching drums and a set of uilleann pipes. Evie picked up the fiddles and managed to break every string with one strum. The 'plink plonk' noises made her laugh as each string snapped. The musicians of the Fairy Rath groaned and sighed as the human child wrecked each fiddle in her eagerness to explore the source of the high-pitched tunes.

Evie turned to the bodhráns and casually put her index finger through each skin, leaving it flapping in the breeze. Then she pretended that the wooded frames were the frames of glasses as she held one up to each eye, sang her usual song of, 'BA DA BOOO, DA BE DA BOOO!' and danced around for a while. Then, bored with her 'glasses', she tossed them aside and picked up the pipes. She squeezed the bellows and the instrument made a sound like a cow having a baby. This made Evie roar with laughter and so she squeezed harder and harder until bag, bellows, chanter, regulators, drones and all the other bits that made up the pipes were in pieces on the ground. She studied the broken parts for a moment, trying to get them to make the funny sound again, but they were now silent. Evie wasn't happy that her funny 'toy' was broken. She looked at General Stump as if it was his fault and walked towards him. King Colm hid behind a tree and the general began to sweat.

## Chapter Nineteen

# Wild Goose Chase

The man, the boy and the she-wolf quickened their step. Finn was feeling anxious after the bird attack. He kept scanning the sky for any sign of the dreaded Sluagh, the horde of raven-like birds that his grandfather had warned him about. He was also curious about the other 'shadow' in the sky, the one Granda said he shouldn't fear, one that could be a *help* to the travellers. It was all so confusing. He had learned by now that all was not what it seemed in this strange land, but for all his Granda's certainty, Finn was beginning to wonder how they would ever get his baby sister back.

It was the thought of Evie that caused his eyes to sting a bit, and a hard lump form in his throat. Finn tried to smile. Mum always told him to do that when he was feeling worried or upset. "It'll make your face feel better," she said. But Finn couldn't smile just now. He had to concentrate hard to stay on the narrow path and to keep up with his grandfather. He fixed his eyes on the old man's strong back, suddenly feeling better as he thought about the way Granda had got them out of some sticky situations and always seemed to be there to stand up for him. Yes, the path was narrow; yes, the drop on the other side was steep. Yes, there were strange shadows and all manner of other scary creatures in this weird and wonderful place, but they were on a mission, a very important mission. Granda was up ahead and he had Aileen at his heels, making sure he didn't fall behind. Slowly Finn realised the corners of his mouth were turning upwards after all.

The pathway along the cliff edge eventually led down to flat land by the sea. It was rocky and Finn found himself slipping and sliding on the loose shale and pebbles. The three kept up their speedy pace, nonetheless. Suddenly Finn noticed small dark dots in the sky. Shielding his eyes from the sun with one hand, he looked up and gulped. The sky was quickly turning black. One moment there was an eerie silence and then the sound of squawking and flapping as hundreds upon hundreds of black dots made up a thick cloud, rapidly coming towards them. Granda had seen them too and the hair on Aileen's back stood on end as she emitted a low growl.

Granda scanned the landscape, looking for a place of safety.

"Get to the trees!" he yelled, pointing to a small clump of fir trees just a short distance away. The three ran as hard as they could but before they could reach cover, big black birds circled close overhead, weaving in and out, around and above, making a terrible 'CAWWWW!' sound. Granda pushed Finn behind him and raised his Shillelagh.

"Cover your eyes, boy, these devils want you blind!" Alieen's ears were pinned back, her head low to the ground and her teeth bared. The birds came fast and close. They looked bigger than the one that had attacked Finn earlier in the day. There was something unnatural about them, something deadly. With feathers shiny and black as an oil slick, and their terrible beaks blacker still, they fixed their unblinking eyes on their prey as they swooped and dive-bombed the three.

Granda swung his stick wildly, sometimes hitting two or three of them with one swing. Aileen snapped and bit, shaking each bird in her teeth, but for each one she caught, ten more appeared, pecking with their hard beaks until they ripped and tore her fur and skin.

Finn saw blood on his Granda's forehead and could feel the sting where beaks had stabbed at his arms as he held them high to shield his face and head. It was hard not to panic, but he knew his grandfather and Aileen were doing their best to protect him. The old man kept swinging his mighty Shillelagh and the she-wolf bit and pawed at the birds, at times crushing them to the ground, but there were so many – too many!

Granda was breathing harder now. Finn feared his swings were getting slower and he was not hitting as many of the attacking birds. Finn had not imagined that his grandfather could be weakened.

He crouched low into a ball, hiding his face, but glanced over at Aileen when she yelped under a particularly harsh blow. The fur on her back was marked with deep red patches of blood. Finn saw the old man look into the wolf's eyes. Their faces said the same thing and Granda's words confirmed it, "There are too many, we can't beat them alone . . ."

"Granda! What can we do?" Finn cried out. "They will kill us!" He was trembling and tears were running down his face. The old man looked down at his grandson. But if Finn had expected terror and desperation, what he saw in his grandfather's eyes was something different.

"The Sluagh are too many for us to beat on our own boy . . . but we are not on our own!"

Suddenly it grew even darker. The evil Sluagh kept trying to peck at his hands and legs, but now there was something else. Finn could almost *feel* the shadow that now engulfed them. Then, a small breeze began to blow his hair. It was hardly anything, but its presence made Finn forget about the Sluagh for a second. It felt calming, even comforting and . . . strong . . . really, really strong. Finn felt a strange thrill of excitement. Then, a great blast of wind forced Finn, Granda and Aileen to the damp earth as the black birds were sent spinning into the trees, their cawing sounds now sounding like their own strangled death cries.

Then . . . darkness.

Finn lay in the dirt. He and his companions could still hear the Sluagh cawing and pecking, but the sound was muffled. It reminded Finn of the time he'd had an ear infection and Mum had put drops and cotton wool in his ears. Instinct made him reach out. It was as though they were completely surrounded by something. Tentatively, Finn pressed into what felt like a protective wall around him. It was warm, alive and felt soft, like feathers. He looked up and first saw Granda smiling and Aileen licking calmly at her wounds. Suddenly a long serpentine neck moved around the inside of the cacoon, and Finn could make out a face. He saw Granda remove his cap and Aileen bow low to the ground. Two black shiny eyes looked at him. They seemed to be set in brownish grey fluffy down – like the soft feathers that had exploded out of his pillow the day he and Dad had that pillow fight (Mum had been really cross about that, but he and Dad hadn't been able to stop laughing). Finn dared to let his eyes stray and saw a long, hard, orange bill and dark crown. The creature was a lot like the geese that sometimes landed near Granda's house, foraging for scraps of bread or fruit; except Finn couldn't imagine how a goose had ever got this large, not even on the rich pickings Gran left out for them.

The size of the face was a little disturbing, but when she spoke, her voice was the calmest sound Finn had ever heard. It reminded him of how his mum would comfort him when he was afraid on dark and stormy nights.

"Ahh . . . Finn, I am Gaoth. I am so glad to be here with you today."

Finn wasn't sure how to respond, but the sound of the Sluagh outside the 'cave' made him wonder why she was happy to be here today, of all days.

"Pleased to meet you, Gaoth," he stammered politely (it wasn't every day you found yourself in conversation with a giant goose). "I am sorry we have met today when the Sluagh are attacking."

"Oh, you and I have been closer than you think, but this is a beautiful day to meet face to face." Gaoth seemed to smile. Her face occasionally winced with pain and Finn knew that it was because the Sluagh were back and pecking at her. The great goose continued. "You see, I am never far from you, Finn, but it is usually in the worst of times that we need to see our true friends face to face. Now, you have some important work to finish, young man. The work of caring for others is your task on this journey; so, let me finish this small battle so that you can continue!"

With that, the great bird unfurled her neck and opened up one gigantic wing. She made a loud honking noise to the sky and flapped her wing making so much wind that the persistent Sluagh got blown back from the travellers. A few came at them again, their beaks pecking at the air, but Gaoth kept one mighty wing protectively wrapped around them. Finn could see that her dirty brown and white feathers were torn and there were hot scars on her wings where the Sluagh had ripped at her, but Gaoth kept her other wing beating steadily, blowing the evil birds away from the travellers.

As the Sluagh gathered themselves for another attack, Gaoth let out another honking scream to the sky. She took a second to look at the travellers, saying, "Do not fret my friends, I am with you. Not everything that comes from above wants to hurt you!" The great goose moved her left wing to block the attacking Sluagh. It was as if she was a soldier using a shield. Then, more noise. Granda looked upwards to see the sky full of birds.
Finn saw them too and began to worry that there would be too many for even Gaoth to fend off. The swarm got closer and suddenly great birds of prey were plucking the Sluagh out of the air. Wild geese attacked the black birds and pecked them into the ground. Falcons grabbed at them with their talons and even tiny robins and

sparrows flew around them in their hundreds, confusing the Sluagh long enough for an eagle or large owl to grab them with their sharp claws. Magpies and seagulls flocked together and beat at the Sluagh with their wings. Ducks pecked at them with their hard bills. Soon the number of allies outweighed the attackers at least two to one and within fifteen minutes the last of the evil Sluagh were flying back to wherever they came from. The noise of flapping wings, screeching and cawing disappeared into the distance and soon the black dots in the sky were gone. When they were sure it was over, the army of birds perched on branches or sat in the grass in silence.

Gaoth opened her wing and released Granda, Finn and Aileen. Granda bowed his head and, with his cap firmly in his hands, thanked Gaoth for her help. Finn ran his fingers along Gaoth's protective wing, inspecting it closely. The great goose could see that Finn wanted to say something.

''Come on, spit it out!" she said, not unkindly.

Gaoth was very large, bigger than Dad's car for sure. She was not beautiful by any means, almost awkward, and yet she had an air of grace about her. Her feathers were torn, and she bore marks and scars and even her natural colours (a woody brown mixed with grey and off-white) looked rather ordinary. She even seemed a little dirty and unkempt.

Finn spoke in a whisper and said, "You are not what I expected. I am very thankful for your help, but you are different than I imagined."

"How so?" asked Gaoth, with a twinkle in her eye.

"Well, you are untidy, a little bit messy and you even look like you might need a bath."

Granda gulped, put one hand over Finn's mouth and quickly spoke up for his Grandson, "Och, he is just a wee boy, he doesn't really understand about . . ."

"About me?" Gaoth butted in, more firmly now. "He seems to understand perfectly!" The great bird honked and squealed loudly and the robins, falcons, seagulls, sparrows, ducks, magpies, owls and one tough looking pigeon with one eye began to chirp and twitter loudly with her. Granda looked a little concerned that his grandson might have insulted the big goose.

"HA! I am untidy and a little bit messy!" she honked. "I certainly could use a bath and yes, I know, my wounds make me look damaged and tough. I am sometimes loud and pushy and I often ignore what people say and do as I please, but I am more than this." Gaoth's eyes twinkled and she spread her wings wide as she preached. "I can seem aggressive at times, but I'm very protective and sometimes I do the things that you would not expect or want me to. At other times, you might think me too quiet and, I know, I often show up in the most unusual places. I am like the wind. I go where I please, with or without the consent of others . . ."

Finn glanced at his Granda, who was listening open-mouthed.

"Sometimes, I like to remain hidden," Gaoth whispered, with a wink at Finn, "although I am never far away. Best of all, I love to surprise you by being the very thing that you least expect. I love to do things that you never thought would be of any help whatsoever . . . and I love to see your face when you realize I was doing what was best, even though you couldn't see it." She threw her head back and let out a honking-type laugh, then bent low so her bill was almost touching Finn's face. "Well done, Finn, you know me better than most!"

The great bird pulled her mighty wings together causing a breeze that ruffled Finn's hair. Granda and Aileen looked at each other with some confusion. All the birds sang and chirped with something that sounded like laughter as Gaoth's wings drew close to Finn's smiling face. Her flight feathers gently touched his cheeks and her long neck curved downwards until she looked him in the eye.

"Finn, I am so glad that you can see me through the eyes that believe. I am all you said and more. Do you know why I am messy, untidy, unkempt, scarred, wounded and looking a little worse for wear? Do you know why I am loud and noisy, a little impolite and rough? Do you know why I am sometimes quiet?"

Finn smiled. He felt no fear at all as he replied with a question, "Because you get to be like the people you are with?"

Gaoth threw her head back, opened her great wings and with a mighty squawk, laughed for a full ten minutes as every bird joined her.

"YES! YES! YES! And, oh, how I love to be with them!" she laughed. "I love all who live beneath my flight path. I love the ones who think they have it right, for it is just a matter of time before they find out that they do not and see the real truth. Ah, but the broken ones and the fearful . . . those who have nothing . . . those who know the struggles of life." Gaoth's vigour was now replaced by such compassion it brought that hard lump back into Finn's throat. Gaoth went on lovingly. "There are those who give up everything for justice and peace . . . the ones who love the outcasts and the beggars and the ones that no-one understands. Yet, it is those who most often sing the song of truth. They are the ones who few choose to befriend, the ones on the fringes but oh, they are the most fun, the best company and the finest of friends."

The boy, the man and the wolf listened in silence as Gaoth continued in a voice so soothing it was like raw cake mixture licked straight from the bowl.

"Finn, listen to your grandfather, he can teach you much. Old man, listen to your grandson, he can teach you also. Both of you learn from the wolf, for she is pure and knows her purpose. Now you must go, you have important business to attend to."

Finn looked at the majestic bird and asked, "Can you come with us and help us?"

Gaoth seemed to smile and replied, "I always do, Finn. I am with you always."

And with that, she beat her mighty wings and flew high into the sky, followed by the rest of the bird army. Soon she was out of sight and her little followers were just specks in the bright blue sky.

Finn looked at Granda. "Didn't she just say she would be coming with us?" he said, confused.

Granda's eyes were still fixed on the sky when he smiled and whispered, "I suspect she just went ahead."

Chapter Twenty

# Nap Time

Evie was bored. She had eaten all the fruit, drunk all the milk and licked up all the honey from King Colm's store. She had beaten and bruised the army, wrecked all the musician's instruments and caused a fair bit of damage to the royal chambers. She hadn't meant to, of course. She was just being playful, and to her, the little fairy people were a source of great amusement. Now she sat on the green grass with her chubby legs out in front of her, talking to her toes. Her mouth twisted into a crooked smile and she half laughed, half burped and completely dribbled as she surveyed the mess around her.

General Stump noticed that her eyelids seemed to be getting heavy and whispered to the king, "I have a plan. She seems to be getting very tired. Let's have some of the musicians sing a lullaby and perhaps she will fall asleep and we can restrain her!"

"Brilliant!" replied the king. "Do it!"

General Stump tiptoed towards the musicians of the Rath. Every now and then Evie's eyes opened wide, causing him to stop dead in his tracks in case she decided to pick him up and throw him into a tree or something. Finally, he reached the singers and instructed an impish little sprite to sing the most calming fairy lullaby that he knew. The little man nodded and took a step up onto an old tree stump that they sometimes used as a stage when they held concerts in the Rath. He adjusted his coat, stood upright and took a big gulp of air as he began to sing an enchantingly sweet refrain,

*"The day is tired and dimming*
*The sun must have its rest,*
*The birds have finished singing*
*As they settle in their nest.*
*And all our labour finished*
*The time to work is done*
*It's time to lay our heads down*
*Just like that setting sun."*

Evie's eyes were almost closed.

"Keep going!" whispered General Stump. "Keep going!"

The little singer continued,

*"Now cows and sheep are resting*
*The horse has lain down,*
*And just the sound of gentle wind*
*Shakes barley on the ground.*
*The bees collect no pollen,*
*The spider's web is spun,*
*It's time to lay our heads down*
*Just like that setting sun."*

A dull thud synchronized with the final word of the song as Evie fell to one side, fast asleep.

General Stump breathed a long sigh of relief, and then gave the command, although he did so in an urgent whisper: "Find our strongest ropes and tie her hands and feet to a tree before she wakes up and causes more damage!"

The little soldiers carefully obeyed.

Chapter Twenty-One

# Tara Hill

Granda took Finn by the shoulders and looked him over. There were a few scratches and small nicks but nothing too serious.

"How are you feeling, lad?" Finn ran his fingers over his chest and arms. Apart from the odd sore bit, he was OK. The old man took off his neckerchief and dipped it into the nearby stream. Aileen was licking her wounds. They were mostly small tears in her skin and coat, but she did have one large gash on her left side and a Sluagh had managed to tear out one of her claws. Granda took the wet cloth and held it on her side until the bleeding stopped. Then he bound her wounded paw with the neckerchief.

"Thank you, brave Aileen, we would have been done for without you today. We need to go to Tara and there may be more trouble, but you owe us nothing. You should rest and heal for a while."

The she-wolf looked at the old man and boy as her human face began to show once again. She spoke in hushed tones. "Wounds and scars are part of life. They prove that we have been on an important quest; they show us that we have really lived! They do not stop us from completing the quest but simply remind us of what it cost to finish it."

The old man nodded in agreement as Aileen returned to her canine form, took a deep breath and got back up on her paws.

"OK then. Are you ready, Finn? The Rath of Colm is only a short walk now. Be ready, the king will not give up his prize without a fight." Finn nodded and they set off once again. It did not take long until they could see Tara Hill and the woodland around it. It was green and lush and quite majestic. Trees grew all around and, as they got closer, Finn felt they were inside a canopy of woven leaves.

Soon they came to a large mound of grass encircled by big oak trees. Each tree had a little door. The place reminded Finn of the paddock settlement where he had been given his boots and trousers, except this place was a big mess! Something had happened here. Broken wooden carts lay on one side and the remnants of fruits, like apple cores and strawberry tops, littered the ground. Spilled milk made little streams in the dirt and the trees and grass were smeared in something sticky and sweet smelling. Broken musical instruments were scattered everywhere and tables and tiny chairs were smashed and broken into splinters.

Finn was uneasy. "What terrible thing has happened here?'' he asked, almost to himself.

"Your sister! That's what!" answered a squeaky voice that came from behind one of the trees. Suddenly a small man leapt out and landed in the centre of the mound. Finn thought that it was an impressive jump for such a small man.

It was King Colm, and he continued with his rant.

"Your sister has been nothing but trouble since she got here. Eating all our food, wrecking my house, beating up my soldiers and destroying our musical instruments. She's a menace!"

"Told you," said Granda, as he winked and nodded at Finn.

Finn found the courage to speak. "Well, why did you keep her here then? Why didn't you send her back home? If she isn't what you want, why is she still here?"

The little monarch laughed hysterically and replied, "She is not for me, you silly boy. I have no need of a human child. We told the changelings that tale because they are simple but fearful. They would not have done the work for us if they had known the truth!"

Granda's eyes narrowed. "And what *truth* would that be, wee man?'

The king looked a little troubled as he answered. "Och, what need do I have of a queen? I rule here alone and have no one telling me what to do. I have more interest in gold and I was promised one hundred pots of it if I captured the girl. It is not me that wants her," King Colm hesitated a little before saying, "It is Caorthannaugh who desires the child!"[20]

Aileen let out a terrifying howl and Granda's face turned pale.

20. Caorthannaugh, pronounced 'Queer-haw-nock' – The mother of evil.

"Caorthannaugh? Didn't St. Patrick himself defeat her? What would she want with my granddaughter? If this is true, I will skin you alive myself, ya wee hallion!"

The little king laughed and said, "You would need to get close to me first!"

Then, Finn heard a familiar sound. It was the noise his baby sister often made when she first awoke. Where was the sound coming from? Finn scanned the woodland and there, behind a big oak tree, he saw Evie tied tightly to the trunk. Finn felt an anger growing within him that he had never experienced before as he turned to Colm and yelled, "You can't have my sister!"

Suddenly little men began to jump into the grassy mound and surround the king. They were each armed with swords, shields and tiny bows and arrows. The king laughed. "Come on then, take her back . . . if you think you can."

But the king didn't laugh for long. In a split second, Aileen's fangs were within inches of his neck. The soldiers moved quickly though and Finn watched in horror as at least twenty soldiers climbed on her and began stabbing and cutting at her ears and back. She winced and shook her body in the way a dog does after it has been swimming. Tiny troops flew off in every direction, but by now, the king was guarded more heavily. Granda joined the assault and, using his walking stick like a golf club, he sent little men flying into the woods, up against trees and flat on their backs. At General Stump's command, tiny archers fired in unison and, even though most of the arrows barely penetrated Granda's clothes, one or two became embedded in his hand and neck. Finn was working out how best to help his companions when he saw a terrifying but familiar sight. Six pairs of bright red eyes were looking at him from deep in the forest. Worse than that, though, was the chill that ran up his spine at the quiet, but deeply penetrating low moaning cry of a woman.

As Granda and Aileen fought the fairy army, six enormous Cu Sidhe came, stealth-like, out of the dark woods and began to circle Finn. Aileen immediately picked up the scent and turned her attention from the king. She spun around and leapt at one of the terrifying dog-like creatures, sinking her sharp fangs deep into its neck. Immediately, another one turned on her and a terrible wrestling match began as they kicked up dirt and sod. Granda looked in horror as the other four fairy hounds circled Finn, but he could do nothing to help as hordes of little soldiers climbed on him and pricked him with their swords. Finn could hear the growls of the Cu Sidhe as they tightened the circle around him. Sweat formed on his face as fear gripped him. He squeezed his eyes shut and stuck his thumb in his mouth like he did sometimes when he thought no-one was looking. He could smell the foul breath of the demon dogs. It was like rotten fish and meat. Yet, terrifying as they were, his mind's eye was some distance away in the woods on the bewitching woman with the dark, dark eyes and the red, red lips. Hope drained from him as she began to float towards him. Time seemed to halt.

It was the strangest thing. Finn was aware of the chaos around him – Granda fighting the tiny soldier army, Aileen wrestling with the terrifying Cu Sidhe, the other four hounds surrounding him with their hungry eyes. Yet somehow, all was still, like he was in a strange bubble. Except he wasn't alone.

Finn felt tears running hot down his cheeks as the woman's face came close to his.

"Banshee! I know why you are here," he said, his voice strangled with sobs. "You are the one who tells us when we are to die. The dogs will have me, won't they?"

The woman smiled and answered, "Not everything is what it seems, Finn. I am the one who warns of the coming of death, but there are many kinds of death. Today you must face one of them." Finn's eyes widened in terror as the beautiful, terrible woman continued. "What will you do now, Finn? Save your sister, or be afraid of your circumstances?"

The young boy looked around him – fangs, claws, swords, arrows and wounded friends. He felt fear rise even more within him, but then heard his sister cry again.

"EVIE! I need to save my sister!" he shouted.

The woman smiled and gently whispered, "Good choice. So, take my hand. It is time for the fear to die!"

As Finn gripped the pale white hand of the Banshee, she began to cry and sob and sing a song,

*"Even you must have your place,*
*Even you have worth,*
*You help us fight, you help us run*
*For all our days on earth*
*But you cannot control us*
*Tho you may often try*
*For if you do, then we proclaim*
*Today, Fear, you must die!"*

She gazed into Finn's eyes and he saw a tear run down her face as she said, "Every death has a sadness and pain. A sense of loss and sorrow, but death has also freedom and release!"

The Banshee opened her red, red lips and screamed a long and wailing moan. This time, it seemed as if everyone could hear it and Finn realised that he felt no fear . . . none at all. His hands reached into the grass as he wrapped them around his fists and whispered, "Angel Blades!" With one swing of his right arm, he knocked every one of the dark hounds on its tail. They regained their footing and attacked as a pack, but Finn was too fast for them. He leapt to his feet and his right fist caught one of the beasts in its red eye, making it whimper and run off. A left hook knocked the second dog into a triple somersault before it hit a tree and then the ground. The remaining two Cu Sidhe looked nervous but stood side-by-side, teeth bared and eyes blazing. They leapt in unison, but Finn raised both hands and slammed their heads deep into the grassy sod, leaving them neck deep in the ground with back legs kicking wildly.

Aileen was still in a bloody fight with the last of the dark hounds as Finn lent a hand (actually a grassy fist) to aid her. Soon the final hound was on the run and Finn and Aileen ran to help Granda. Finn found another use for his leprechaun boots as he cleared a path to his grandfather by kicking little soldiers far into the woods, as Aileen grabbed them in her jaws and flung them in the other direction. Soon the three surrounded King Colm as General Stump ran and hid behind the dung heap.

Looking around for any other imminent attack, Finn noticed the Banshee nearing the edge of the woods. She still floated, her white body ghost-like against the dark of the trees. Her eyes were fixed on Finn. Now, though, her once twisted red lips formed the shape of a deep smile and she waved to Finn before turning and disappearing into the firs.

He remembered the words of Gaoth and knew they were true. Not everything is as it seems, and sometimes the most unexpected thing is what is best for us. Granda's voice interrupted his thoughts.

"Finn, get Evie!"

Finn sped over to where his sister was tied to the tree. Evie let out a cry for a second then, stretched, and broke every rope. She saw her brother and screamed, "KEE KEE!" Before he knew it, Finn was engulfed in a slobbery kiss. His little sister seemed quite undisturbed by the whole episode!

Meanwhile, King Colm looked nervous. "Look, if it was just me, I would have sent her back," he stammered. "She's a menace and very strong for a baby. I have no use for her. I just wanted some gold. You can't blame a king for that can you?" he said pleadingly, looking first at Finn, then at Granda.

"Oh, I blame you alright, you greedy wee hallion," said Granda, his face menacingly close to Colm's. "What does Caorthannaugh want with my granddaughter?"

The king's expression changed, and he seemed to be looking past the old man.

"Well, you can ask her yourself!" he replied.

Aileen growled and they all turned to see a gigantic shape rise high above the trees. First it looked like a swirling cloud of smoke, but soon it began to take the form of a gigantic woman. Her head was covered in something that looked more like fire than hair and her skin was black and white. Her long arms waved around her in some kind of macabre dance and glowing red lines shone through her skin as if her veins ran with fire instead of blood. Her eyes glowed red like the Cu Sidhe and her body was draped in black smoke that fitted around her like a moving, living dress. Finn carried Evie to his Granda's side as they all stared at the gigantic woman.

"Granda, what is that?"

"She is Caorthannaugh," Granda whispered with a tremor in his voice. "The oldest evil in all of Ireland . . . in fact, the oldest evil anywhere!"

For a moment, Caorthannaugh fixed her terrifying eyes on the baby girl, now clinging to her brother. The witch's mouth twisted in a cruel snarl and fire dribbled from it like saliva made from molten lava. Then she spoke, with hissing sounds attached to her words.

"Colm! What is thisssss? Why is the girl with the othersssss? You have failed me, little man!"

With that, she threw back her head and made an awful choking sound. The creature coughed and spluttered then looked at the king. He hardly had time to beg for mercy when Caorthannaugh spat a ball of fire at him and the little man was no more. Then the monster looked to the sky and screamed like a thousand banshees. The sound made every woodland creature scurry away and the flying ones take to the sky. Granda yelled, "RUN!" and the four headed for the trees.

The fire spitter's head turned to see the companions fleeing and instantly puked a stream of boiling lava in their direction. The molten fluid burned up trees, grass and even rocks and stones.

"SHE'SSSSS MINE!" it screamed as the swirling smoke twisted and she followed her prey. Granda picked Finn up and put him on his shoulders while Evie rode on the back of Aileen and giggled as if it was all a great game. Fire, like drops of burning rain, dripped all around them as Caorthannaugh gave chase. Trees ignited and plants and flowers turned to charred black ash with every step the monster took.

Soon Granda, Finn and Aileen were exhausted (Evie was pulling Aileen's fur, giggling and trying to make her run faster). They came to a large rock face. There was nowhere to run. Caorthannaugh drew closer and smiled menacingly.

"The girl issssss mine. Give her to me and you may all go home sssssafely!" Granda looked at the beast and answered her with his chin jutted out and his face firm. "What is it you want with her? Why is Evie so important to you?"

"Every child issss sssspecial to me, but sssssome are alssso a threat to every sssssscheme I have. Sssssome of them are more important than they will ever know. The girl issss important to me becausssse ssshe isss important to the boy!" Granda shook his head and looked her in the eye.

"Seriously? So, you'd take a child as hostage so that you can do your evil work? You aren't so powerful or great. You are just a thief, a liar and a kidnapper. You are pathetic!" Finn didn't know how Granda had the guts to talk like this. He watched the gigantic woman as her flaming red eyes burned with rage. In an instant, her hand swept down and plucked the old man up. She held him close to her face and slowly whispered, "I think I ssssshall eat you, old man!"

She opened her jaws and Granda could see that her throat looked like a fiery pit as she began to move him towards it. The heat was almost unbearable and Granda could feel his clothes beginning to singe. Finn looked on with horror and Aileen howled a mournful moan. Even Evie had begun to realise that things were not good and began to whimper a little. It was then that Finn remembered the words of Gaoth. Without a second thought, Finn began to scramble up the rock face as fast and as high as he could. Evie whimpered as Aileen licked her face to calm her. Soon, Finn was almost level with the fire monster's face and the hand that held his Granda.

Finn screamed, "I am not afraid of you Caorthannaugh!" He leapt from the rock face and grabbed the beast's wrist with both arms.

Caorthannaugh looked in surprise as the boy climbed over beside his Grandfather. "I had planssss to corrupt you and usssse you for my own endsssss, Finn. You are more important than you know . . . but I sssssuppose I will have to sssettle for devouring you!"

The old man looked at his grandson with tears in his eyes. "Jump, Finn, save yourself!"

But Finn had no fear. His face was full of strength and determination as he replied, "Granda, remember what Gaoth said . . . she said that it is often in the worst of times that we need to see our true friends, face to face!"

A breeze began to waft at the fire around them and then in a mighty wind, the fire demon looked up and saw Gaoth high above.

"Foolissssh bird. Don't you know that wind just fansssss my flamessssss!" She opened her mouth as wide as she could and placed the old man and boy on her burning tongue.

The man and boy clung together in a hug; the kind of hug that made you think nothing could hurt you. They whispered the very same words in each other's ears, "I love you!" as the fire spitter's mouth closed.

For a few seconds, everything went quiet, except for whimpers from Aileen and Evie shouting frantically, "KEE KEE! POPPY POP!"

The burning beast smiled with an evil glee, looking at the girl and wolf as if she was deciding if she should eat them too, when suddenly her face contorted. Her arms began to stiffen, and she made a horrible gagging sound. She began to choke and Aileen, fearing the beast was going to spit fireballs at them just as she had done to King Colm, herded Evie to safer distance. The monster twitched and screamed, then her mouth opened, revealing Finn holding his Granda in a piggyback as the thick soles of his brilliant leprechaun boots kept the heat of the monster's tongue at bay. It was a long way to the ground, but Caorthannaugh used one long finger to scrape the two off her burning tongue and out into the air. Finn and his Granda hurtled to the ground but, instead of a nasty bump on the stones below, they found themselves landing softly on unkempt feathers as Gaoth swooped down to catch them on her back.

Caorthannaugh coughed and choked more, as splashes of red flame and vile green ooze gushed from her mouth. She held her throat with both hands and then, with a terrible scream, she shrunk into her own black cloud, smaller and smaller until everyone could see how small she really was. Gaoth gently landed on the ground below and the man, the boy, the girl, the wolf and the goose embraced for a long time.

Chapter Twenty-Two

# Homeward Bound

The long embrace came to an end when Evie scampered off to chase a grey squirrel that she noticed returning to his home in the forest. Gaoth smiled (even though she had a hard beak, she seemed to have the ability to smile) and watched Evie as she tried to scale the tree after the little creature.

"She is a little menace for sure," she said, "but a very important little menace!" Granda, Finn and Aileen all nodded in agreement. The goose continued, "Her ordeal with Colm didn't bother her too much, but every child who has been taken needs some special attention for a time. Perhaps more hugs than usual. Evie has the blood of that old rapscallion Finn McCool flowing through her. You should avoid picking a fight with that one!" Finn looked at his sister and smiled. He had always thought that she was far too strong for a baby girl. He turned to Gaoth, majestic and proud, ruffled and dirty, scarred and wounded, awkward and graceful. She was so much more than he had ever imagined. Goath tilted her head to one side, smiled at the boy and said once again, "Spit it out!"

Finn laughed and said, "What happened? Why are we not in the belly of the beast? Did you do that, Gaoth? Did you make it choke?"

The great bird stretched her wings out for a second and shook her head. "Well, I am glad you wish to give me some credit, Finn, but in truth I only guided you. It was you who overcame; you and your Granda. Caorthannaugh only seeks to devour and destroy. Her heart is filled with hate and she feeds on guile, bitterness and lies, but there is one thing that she cannot stomach. So, tell me this and tell me no more, do you remember the last words you both said as she closed her jaws?"

Finn and Granda replied together, "I love you!"

Goath threw her head back and honked to the sky and laughed, "YES! YES! LOVE is the one thing Caorthannaugh cannot stomach!"

Laughter filled the air as birds, mice, squirrels, spiders, foxes and rabbits returned to the forest to join in the joy that was almost tangible. Gaoth looked at her friends and said, "Well, I must fly and you should be heading home. We shall meet again, my friends!" With two powerful flaps of her great wings, she took off and soon was so high that no one could see her, but they could still feel the gentle breeze of her wings.

After a moment or two, Granda spoke up. "Well, I suppose we are done here. Time to get back home!" Evie lifted both arms up for she had obviously decided that she was not walking, and Aileen was glad that she was not sitting on her back and pulling her fur. The old fella flipped the little girl onto his shoulders and the four set off back towards home. It had taken days to get to Tara, but they made better time on the way back without the distraction of Selkies, Kelpies and the like. Eventually they were at the edge of the forest and Finn could see the old VW car.

In the final miles Finn had swapped places with his sister, riding high on his Granda's shoulders, and Evie had nestled down in the fur on Aileen's back. She climbed off now, pulled the wolf's ears and kissed her face, much to Aileen's annoyance as it changed her back into human form.
She looked at her companions and spoke.

"It is time for me to return to my kind. Thank you for allowing me to go on the quest." Finn was concerned about her wounds. They still looked red and sore, but the she-wolf told him not to worry. "They are reminders of our adventure together. They are a part of my story, our story. They will heal in time. I will treasure the scars; they tell me that I am always being healed. I think we will meet again my young friend, there are more adventures ahead for you, boyo . . . and your menace of a sister!" Finn gave the wolf a hug and kiss, and Granda nodded and smiled as her face turned back to the visage of a wolf and she sped off into the deep thick woods.

Once the children were strapped into their seats, Granda turned the ignition key and the old VW burst into life with a splutter and a bang. Soon they were driving back home to Wexford.

Chapter Twenty-Three

# Wexford in the Morning

Evie was asleep in no time at all and Finn felt his eyes growing heavy. He slipped his thumb into his mouth, hoping that Granda couldn't see. The landscape soon grew familiar – small winding roads lined with tall green hedges or rough grey stone walls; villages with Irish Pubs, cold grey churches and quaint teashops; white cottages with red doors, stables, green post boxes and road signs written in Irish and English. All whizzed past in a blur as they drove along in the rusty blue Beetle.

"Still sucking that old thumb of yours, boyo?" laughed Granda. Finn's face turned a little pink; he knew that he was too old to keep the habit. Then, to his surprise, his Granda continued, "Don't ever stop lad, it's an important thing to do!" Finn wasn't sure what that meant, but he was happy that he wasn't being scolded. The old fella went on, "Aye, that ancestor of ours sucked his thumb his whole life after he touched the Salmon of Knowledge with it. It helped him figure things out when he needed to. You keep it up, lad; you will need all the wisdom that you can muster!"

Finn had to ponder on that one. Had Granda really said 'Salmon of Knowledge'? He would ask.

There was bound to be another great story here, but for now . . .

Finn's head nodded forward and he dropped into sleep.

Finn awoke to the rumble of the car along the rough coast road that led through Courtown Harbour and on to Granda's house. Granda parked the car in front of number 9 and Evie woke up the second the engine switched off. Finn ran into the house first as Granda unstrapped Evie from her seat. Gran was standing at the top of the stairs and swept him off his feet as he reached her. She kept kissing his head and checking his face, ears, arms and legs as if looking for damage.

"Are you alright? Did you get Evie? Is your old Granda still in one piece? I've been worried sick, y'know."

Granda walked upstairs with Evie on his shoulders.

"POPPY POP! POPPY POP," sang Evie, waving her arms wildly in the air and nearly knocking Granda's ears off in her excitement.

Gran gave them a group hug, then looked at Granda and said, "You old eejit. Taking on the fairies at Tara were ye? And I suppose there were Cu Sidhes to deal with?"

Granda nodded.

"And other kinds of devils that cause mischief?"

Granda nodded again but Finn yelled, "And Selkies, a Kelpie and . . ."

"Och, now that's enough Finn. Your gran doesn't need all the details!"

"Oh, I think I do!" She gave Granda a very stern look and said, "Go on, Finn."

"Well we met The Amadán, a Lephrechaun, a Conriocht . . ."

Gran muttered, "A Conriocht is good."

" . . . there were Sluagh," continued Finn, rubbing his arm where a peck mark was still stinging a little. Gran glared at Granda. " . . . oh, and this horrible thing called Caorthannaugh!"

Gran gasped. "Caorthannaugh! How did you come across that devil?"

"It's a long story, dear. Why don't we just have a cup of tea and we will tell you all about it?" said Granda, heading to the kitchen.

Finn chirped in, " . . . and don't forget Gaoth, Granda!"

Gran smiled when she heard the wild goose's name, but then shook a fist at her husband and kissed him on the cheek. "I am glad you are all safe. I am thankful for the Conriocht and especially for Gaoth . . . but the Caorthannaugh! What were you thinking?" Gran continued to mutter as she stomped into the kitchen, her big feet banging on the worn wooden floorboards.

Soon the table was full of all kinds of food and drinks and Finn wondered if they ever had 'just a cup of tea' in this house. Granda and Finn told the whole story to Gran who looked horrified, proud and startled at the same time. Evie ate bread and tried to lick jam off her own elbow. After she had heard the entire saga, Gran sighed and said, "Never again, you three! Any trouble that comes this way again is to be avoided at all costs." She winked at Finn. "And if it can't be avoided, then you better bring me along with you. Somebody has to be the grown up!" Finn laughed as Granda looked like a little boy being scolded. Gran could stare better than Evie and she gave him the full weight of her reprimand now.

"You will need to tell their mum, y'know!"

"Och, what she doesn't know won't hurt her, dear!"

"NO! The truth. You will tell her everything. That is how we do things in this family, right?"

"She will be angry."

"Aye, and who could blame her," said Gran, shaking her head disapprovingly.

Granda nodded and whispered, "You are right. I will talk with her when she gets back."

"Good! Now it's time that tired children were in bed, and tired Grandas!"

Soon all was dark and quiet in the little house, except for very contented snoring sounds.

Chapter Twenty-Four

# All Together Now

Breakfast was the usual fare of soda bread, bacon, eggs, tea, orange juice and more. Evie smiled and dived in right away. Finn and Granda watched her for a while, but thankfully, her eyes stayed dark brown until she was eventually full of food and giggles and burps. Gran picked up plates and cups and carried them into the kitchen as the sound of a car engine shuddered to a stop outside the house.

"We're home!" yelled Mum, as Dad carried the cases into the house. Both children ran to hug their parents and Mum kissed and squeezed them for a full ten minutes.

"So, what have you kids been doing?"

The children looked at their grandparents and Granda said, "Well, it's been a busy time!' Gran gave him a look and he continued. "We need a wee talk, darlin'!"

Mum looked at the old man and said in a low voice, "Dad?"

They walked out into the garden and closed the big glass door. Finn could see his mum fold her arms in the way she did when she was annoyed with him or his sister. Every now and then they heard her saying, "Sluagh?" or "Conriocht?" as she wagged her finger at her father.

After a little while, Finn saw them hug before they came back inside. Mum held her children once again. She looked at Gran and they both shook their heads before Mum said, "That's quite a story, but you know, I am glad that you were both here. Thank you for taking care of the children."

Finn's dad came in and asked, "So, what exciting things have you kids been doing?'

The room fell silent.

Chapter Twenty-Five

# Time To Go Home

The final day in Wexford was relaxed and refreshing after the big adventure. Mum and Dad packed cases while Granda and Gran took the children for walks in the forest and by the beach (with a stern warning from Mum to 'stay out of trouble'). There was, of course, lots of good things to eat, and Gran chased Evie around the trees as Finn and Granda walked and talked.

"Granda, how did Mum seem to know what you were talking about yesterday? Did you tell her stories when she was a little girl?"

Granda smiled and nodded before answering, "Well I did tell her stories when she was small, but your mother also has the blood of the McCools running through her veins. She has been on some adventures too."

Finn shook his head. "Mum? My mum? Next you will be telling me that Dad is a superhero and Uncle Gary is a warrior!"

The old man smiled again.

"Your dad *is* a superhero. He has a Father's love inside him and that is one of the most powerful forces in the universe. As for Uncle Gary, if we ever have trouble with beasties again, I think we need to have him along for the ride. You will be surprised what that young fella can do!"

They stopped to visit Shea's Ice Cream Shop and had large 99s with raspberry syrup. Soon they were back home, where Dad had already packed the luggage in the car.

"OK we need to set off back to Alba," said Mum as she brushed her long blonde hair.[21] "Kiss your grandparents, kids. And say thank you for everything . . . well, almost everything." Her reflection in the mirror gave Granda a cheeky look.

The children were wrapped in a giant bear hug with their grandparents when suddenly Granda shouted, "Oh! Is there anything from the wee people in the plum tree?"

Evie and Finn dashed outside to find packets of sweets by the Plum tree door. A tiny hand-written note said,

**"Thank you for visiting us again. We hope you come back and have a better rest next time! Love from the Plum Tree Wee People."**

Finn smiled as he read the note and Evie ripped open her bag of sweets, dropped them in the grass but ate them anyway. Finn looked at Granda and said, "I know that you leave the sweets and notes here for us, but I love that you do. I will miss the nice things you do for us, Granda."

21. Alba, another name for Scotland.

The old man looked surprised and said, "Is that so?" as he pointed to the Plum Tree. Finn turned his head just in time to see a tiny hand inside the tree pull the little wooden door shut tight. He looked back at his grandfather and they uttered the same words at the very same time,

"Not everything is what it seems!"

# Glossary

Some of the names and words in this book are in the old Irish language. They can be very tricky to pronounce, so here's some help with how to say them and a bit more about what they mean.

**Alba:** Another name for Scotland. Some people also call it Caledonia.

**Amadán:** Pronounced *Om-a-daun* – 'Dark Fool', like an ancient Irish version of The Joker!

**Banshee:** Pronounced *Ban-she* – A female spirit who needs lots of tissues because cries a lot!

**Bodhrán:** Pronounced *Bow-raun* – An Irish drum. The word probably means 'Skin Tray' (eeeyeww!) because it is made of a wooden circle and goatskin. You beat the drum with a stick called a 'Tipper' and it makes a low thudding sound.

**Caorthannaugh:** Pronounced *Queer-haw-nock* – 'The Mother of Evil'. She's a nasty demon thingy who, according to Irish legend, picked a fight with St. Patrick, but that's another story. (Spoiler alert, Patrick won!)

**Changeling:** Pronounced *Change-ling* – A fairy who changes places with a human. They are smelly because they don't like to wash. They are very greedy eaters and behave very strangely.

**Clurichaun:** Pronounced *Cloor-re-con* – Cousin to the Leprechaun, but this one is a very bad-tempered and selfish male Irish fairy.

**Conriocht:** Pronounced *Con-richt* – an Irish werewolf. They don't just change their minds; they change everything about their appearance. They can be very hairy and probably use a lot of shampoo!

**Cu Sidhe:** Pronounced *Coo-she* – A fairy hound. A really, really big pooch!

**Eejit:** Pronounced *E-jit* – Someone who isn't very wise and does silly things, quite a lot of the time. The kind of person who puts lipstick on their forehead when you ask them to make up their mind!

**Fionn MacCumhaill:** Pronounced *Finn Ma Cool* – A famous Irish warrior hero. Legend has it he built a part of the Giant's Causeway, a place you can go see in County Antrim, Northern Ireland. He was Irish Spitting Champion at one point (Yuk!).

**Farraige:** Pronounced *Far-e-ga* – Beside, or close to, the sea.

**Gaoth:** Pronounced *Ga-wee* – the Irish word for wind.

**Hallion:** Pronounced *Hal-yon* – A disrespectful person who makes bad choices, like eating hot ice-cream or frozen soup. They make everyone else shake their heads a lot!

**Kelpie:** Pronounced *Kel-pee* – A magical shape-shifting water creature, but they mostly look like a horse.

**Leprechaun:** Pronounced *Lep-re-con* – A very tricky, musical, shoe-making, male Irish fairy.

**Rath:** Pronounced, well, *Rath!* – A ring-shaped or circular enclosed fortress. You can still find them all over Ireland. They are often a bit neglected and covered in grass and weeds.

**Selkie:** Pronounced *Sell-kee* – A magical water-creature. A bit like a mermaid, except they really look like a seal.

**Sleekit:** Pronounced *Sle-kit* – Sly or deceitful.

**Sluagh:** Pronounced *Slew-ha* – A horde or a crowd. In this case, of multitude of big, nasty, scary other-worldly pecking birds.

**Tayto:** Pronounced *Tay-toe* – Irish potato crisps (or 'chips' if you're reading this in America). The best potato snacks in the world . . . ever!

# Acknowledgements

As Clarence the Angel tells us in the movie *It's A Wonderful Life,*

*It would be fair to say that it is almost impossible to tell the effect others have on any one life.*

I want to mention one or two – ok, three or four – individuals who have really helped to make this book happen.

I cannot express my gratitude to everyone who inspired, helped and encouraged me to write this book, there are simply too many. Special thanks must to go to my long-suffering wife, Kylie, who has to deal with my moods and quirkiness when I am in 'focused mode'. She gave me space, time and encouragement beyond mere words. Her grace and love towards me are unending.

My children, Debbie and Gary, for loving a father who has never really held down a 'normal' job for most of his life, some may even say has not been normal for most of his life!

My grandchildren Finn and Evie who have given me a new love for life and hope for better things. Thank God for children everywhere: they are not just our future, they are our present reminders of how good life can be when we see magic and wonder in everything.

Mr. Henderson, my high school English teacher who had never heard of dyslexia and told me repeatedly that I was a stuttering idiot who would never amount to anything. Thank you for my reports declaring, 'Samuel must try harder!' This book is testament to the fact that I did.

American author Suzy Parish, for the middle-of-the-night phone calls and constant nudges to keep going.

Malcolm Down and Sarah Grace Publishing for taking a chance on a rather raggedy, slightly dyslexic, Irish yarn-spinner, who likes to shoot from the hip. Thank you for thinking this was good enough to unleash on children everywhere.

Finally, I simply cannot get gushy-wushy enough about my wonderful friend and editor Angela Little. With her help, we raised the bar far beyond anything I could have achieved on my own. Her input, editing skills, insight, experience and belief in me are what has finally brought this little book to fruition. I owe her a pie and a box of something sweet for her expertise and support. (She also plays bass guitar and is a very nice lady!)

# About the Author

Sammy Horner is a husband, father, grandfather, minister, author and musician. He lives in Wexford, Ireland with his wife Kylie, and when he isn't travelling around the world, he loves to have visits from his grandchildren Finn and Evie.